Manifest West

Even Cowboys Carry Cell Phones

Manifest West

Even Cowboys Carry Cell Phones

Western
Press Books

WESTERN PRESS BOOKS
GUNNISON, COLORADO

Manifest West: Even Cowboys Carry Cell Phones Copyright © 2013 by Western Press Books

ISBN: 978-1-60732-289-4 (paperback) 978-1-60732-290-0 (ebook)

Library of Congress Control Number: 2013942860
Published in the United States of America

Western Press Books
Gunnison, Colorado

"Detail of the Four Chambers to the Horse's Heart" by Allen Braden was first published in *Elegy in the Passive Voice* (University of Alaska/Fairbanks) and "Hoof Rot" was first published in *Meridian*.

"Late Harvest" by Ellaraine Lockie first appeared in *Otter Tail Review*. "Rebellion" first appeared in *Your Daily Poem*. "Those Montana Men" first appeared in *Shirt Pocket Book* (broadside), Poets West.

"Letter to Weingarten Written as the Script for an Imaginary Western" by Adam Tavel first appeared in *Connotation Press: An Online Artifact*.

"More . . . Your Gunslinger Shadow Grows Amber" by Red Shuttleworth first appeared in his book *Ghosts & Birthdays* (Humanitas Media Publishing).

"A Rancher's Rainstorm" by Carolyn Dahl first appeared in *Camas* as "Sid's Rainstorm."

"The Cattle" by Leonore Wilson first appeared in her book *Western Solstice* (Hiraeth Press).

"After Chores" by Don Thackrey first appeared in *WestWard Quarterly*.

"The Ranch Woman's Secret" by William Notter first appeared in the chapbook *More Space Than Anyone Can Stand* (Texas Review Press), and later in *Holding Everything Down* (Southern Illinois University Press).

"Burial For Horsemen" by Tom Sheehan first appeared in *Wilderness House Literary Review*.

"Big Horn Passover" by Donna Kaz first appeared in *Lilith*.

"haiku #2" by Sally Clark first appeared in Dos Gatos Press' *Anthology of Southwestern Haiku* and "haiku #3" first appeared online at *USA Today*, August 26, 2003.

"Cowboy Stories" by Michael Shay was first published in a slightly different form in *Owen Wister Review*, titled "Call Me Robert."

"Eight Fragments . . ." by Joe Wilkins first appeared in *The Georgia Review*. Parts of the essay also appeared in a different form in his memoir, *The Mountain and the Fathers: Growing up on the Big Dry* (Counterpoint Press, 2012).

"Feedlot Cowboy" by Robert Rebein first appeared as a chapter in his book *Dragging Wyatt Earp: A Personal History of Dodge City* (Swallow/Ohio UP, 2013).

"Calving Time" by Echo Klaproth first appeared as "A Lesson From Mother Nature" in a slightly different form in *Words Turn Silhouette* (Sagebrush Echoes, 2007).

"Real Cowboy" by Heather Sappenfield first appeared in *Shenandoah*.

"Long After Memory Is Gone" by Rick Kempa was first published in *High Desert Journal*.

EDITOR

TERESA MILBRODT

ASSISTANT EDITORS

REBECCA BISHOP
ALEX JENSEN
BECCA LUBANG
APRIL OLESON
TRISTAN PALMGREN
MAGGIE SAMEK
JORDAN SMITH
KANDRA VOLENTINE
COLE WADSWORTH
SARAH WARD

CONSULTING EDITORS

MICHAELA ROESSNER-HERMAN
MARK TODD
DAVID YEZZI

COVER PHOTOGRAPH

CHRIS ROURKE

COVER AND INTERIOR DESIGN

SONYA UNREIN

CONTENTS

FICTION

ESSAYS

CONTRIBUTORS

Foreword

Like any legendary figure, the cowboy is part myth and part reality, memorialized by history and Hollywood, envied by those who spend days at desks and dream of trading swivel chairs for saddles. The writings in this anthology serve as testament to the cultural love, bordering on obsession, of the American cowboy. These works cover the gamut from the romanticized movie cowboy to ranchers, freelancers, and contemporary wranglers who wear hoodies and work in massive feedlot pens.

The cowboy that emerges from this collection is multi-faceted, as the book juxtaposes longhorns being sprayed at a car wash with cowboys advertising services on Craigslist and Pepsi-drinking cowboys met on Amtrak trains. There are portraits of the old cowboys, crotchety coffee-swigging men with too many stories about how things were better four decades ago. However, the figure remains one constructed of loyalties—loyalty to work, loyalty to family, loyalty to animals, loyalty to the land.

This profession defines the individual because of the level of dedication and commitment required. These jobs are part career and part compulsion but always blend work and life, an avocation that is assumed because one can't not do it. This identity is accepted along with barbed-wire-fence stringing, manure-spreading, and a variety of malodorous tasks that demand the stamina and endurance of a professional athlete, even for those who don't ride bulls. The cowboy still represents the independent be-your-own boss spirit that we like to consider American (though as essayist Robert Rebein points out, much of the jargon has Mexican origins).

This collection also conveys a deep respect for nature and the elements that is owned only by those who have to work in them every day. The cowboy is an unromantic, a part-time scientist and veterinarian who can help a cow during a breech birth, understand the roots of biology, deal with everyday blood, shit, and mud, and know where beef comes from but willingly eat a steak and shrug.

The deep relationship between people and horses is also a prevalent theme in these works, as the horse emerges repeatedly as friend, work partner, and occasional confidant. The close attention and care given to the horse, and the way horses care for their humans in return, speaks to a relationship between animals and people seen in few other lines of work. To some, riding a horse can become an addiction—once you've started, you're hooked. Perhaps this is part of the continued attraction to the cowboy way of life, though like family farms, the family ranch and cowboying as a profession is dying out and making way for large corporate feed lots.

Yet despite this tenuous status, this anthology is a testament to the fact that some people will always continue and cherish this way of life. The image of the cowboy will likewise remain vivid in our imagination, unable to be separated from Western mythology, a means to connect ourselves with the wild and rugged individuals we dream we used to be. In this age of computers and cubicles we want to touch and preserve that history, but we must allow for shifting traditions. Even cowboys carry cell phones.

POETRY

ALLEN BRADEN

Detail of the Four Chambers to the Horse's Heart

1.
Listen. The last time I saw my father
alive, he spoke of horses, the brute geometry
of a broken team in motion. He tallied
the bushels of oats, gallons of water
down to the drop each task would cost.
How Belgians loved hardwood hames the most.
Give them the timber sled at Logging Camp
any day, the workable meadows in need
of leveling, tilling, harrowing, new seeding.
We could've been in our dark loafing shed,
cooling off between loads of chopping hay,
the way he carried on that last good day.
With the proper encouragement, he said,
they would work themselves to death.

2.
Drifts of snow up to their hocks and knees,
the team struggles. They want nothing more
than to droop in the breath-warm barn,
to fill both cheeks with the chopped timothy
of June's first cutting, to muzzle trough water,
then rest. Nothing more now than to rest.
Snowflakes alighting on their hot withers
vanish. The sledge so laden with slush and ice.
They snort, toss, stamp and fart to keep blood
thrumming through their bodies, heavenly
machinery in sync with work and weather.

Because the driver, my father, chirps and barks
in a barely human way, they labor.
Their work will stop when he says so.

3.
Breaker of Mustangs and Broncos, saint
to all things unbridled, you knew cancer
(like the roots dismantling your culvert)
would have you drawn and quartered.
The stallions whipped to sunder limb
from perishable limb. Divided, the evil
in a body loses its power. The fallen
horse, for example, you saw trampled
had disappeared overnight, scattered
across acres by coyotes or not as dead
as you thought. His harem of mares
soon another's. You were often called
a man even then. Name it fate or omen.
Their hooves almost touching the ground.

4.
So much can spook a horse when his world
stirs awake: an unlatched gate the wind
knocks, a pine knot popping like a shotgun
in the campfire. If blinders fail to block
all fresh deadfall along his usual trail,
he'll snap the trace. Now loop a rope
around his upper lip to put a "twitch" on.
This, somehow, settles him down more than
the doubletrees' clink and creak, the routine
caress of your currycomb, the molasses
that glues oats in hunks of giddy bliss.
Given sweets, any horse will follow you.
Whisper what you want to this one.
Never question that disquieted heart.

ALLEN BRADEN

Hoof Rot

When the cold eases through bag balm
to chap and chafe their teats,
when cow shit freezes hard as horn
into ridges along the concrete that cut,
we sort the lame with broomsticks and canes.

This rot is democratic to say the least,
festering the hooves of our gray cattle.
They gimp along in light the color of slush
and let us herd them wherever we want
as if they know their time's almost up.

Under the bare light bulbs of the barn
a winter corralled amounts to sores
that ooze the juices of summer.
Stanchioned, these cattle they rattle the bars
in time with their senile grunts, almost snores.

With a lasso and pair of hoof nippers,
we prune them to the quick,
spray on the vet's antiseptic purple sting
then hobble back to woodstove warmth,
clumsy as old men in our steel-toed boots.

SARAH BROWN-WEITZMAN

Cowboy

Sculpture by Duane Hanson

How tired he seems leaning against the museum wall,
thumbs hooked into the front pockets of his jeans.
Waiting to be called for the next rodeo event,
he tries not to think about his situation. He owns

three shirts, another pair of jeans, this leather bridle,
a new hat and a fake-silver buckle, a month's wages.
He knows he has no future beyond a bunkhouse.
He wishes he could afford a horse of his own.

But how could he keep it in oats? Might another ranch
pay a little more, serve better grub? If he followed
the rodeo trail, what would he do if he were seriously injured
and couldn't compete again? What jobs could he get then?

The roping contest's over. Bull riding's next. He's paid
the $10 entry. He hears his name. He hopes he can hang on.

KATHLEEN WINTER

Longhorn at the Car Wash

Outside a mini-mart, beside a cavernous car wash
      he stands while three men direct fierce spray
   at the speckled plains of his flanks.
      I'm looking down from a bus full of women,
here to see the famous Lost Maples with Mother,

fallen into her golden years. Long as a 60's
      Buick, the steer rearranges his weight as a puddle
   deepens on asphalt, reddened with caliche
      the men take out of his hide. The younger
farmworker wears a white t-shirt, tired boots

like the others, but he stares at the bus as if its
      tinted interior's filled with treasure. Another guy
   yanks the rope so the man with the hose
      gets an angle on the animal's head. The steer
shudders as water hits his nose, his eyes.

Horns stretch miles to each side, to fields
      dwarfing this small-town Valero, sharp tips lifted
   in October air. It seems too ordinary,
      the garrulous grandmothers, city visitors,
all wearing dresses and poised to judge foliage,

then eat broiled chicken at the newest
      French restaurant in the Hill Country, brown
   men outside taxed with shifting elements
      of flesh and water, the steer taller at the shoulder
than any of his handlers, an enigmatic property,

speaking his own tongue to no one.

STEPHEN PAGE

The Bad Guy

In paddock nine a bull grew wings
Flapped and flew over barb wire;
Or did it just step over
A three-foot-high electric fence?

Some months ago your phone decided
Not to lift or ring,
So it could not report natal morning,
Nor answer sunset blackening deaths.

In three weeks you consumed a cow,
Murdered another,
Assassinated a calf: but
Their blood does not brown the grass.

You think with your close-set mercury eyes
That admin is uncountable,
And the two-hour curving highway between us
Will horse you time to town.

I braided a noose out of calf hide,
And carry a nine-millimeter on my hip,
Constructed a yardarm inside my office;
Am sharpening my belt-knife upon my desk.

ELLARAINE LOCKIE

Late Harvest

He meets them for coffee at the Q Cafe in the morning
Men who could have walked out of the Charlie Russell
print on the wall on their bowed legs
Rigged in Stetsons and scuffed cowboy boots
that hide bald heads and bunioned feet
Long-sleeved shirts with snaps and bled-out Levis
that cover long johns even in 100 degrees

Their bull elk demeanors work hard
at making the coffee klatch look like coincidence
It wouldn't be manly to need camaraderie
Accomplices who agree about the new espresso shop
where shots are two bucks each
Some Goddamned California invention
Not like when coffee was
twenty-five cents with free refills

Men who lived the outhouse and cattle rustling story
in the Way Back When column of this week's *Mountaineer*
And drank boiled barley water together
through the Depression

Moving into town close to the medical and senior
centers might have been the right thing he tells himself
But work ethics speak louder than shooting the bull
even if his son won't hear of it

So after an hour he climbs in his truck
and heads for the ranch
Carrying his rifle, an expired driver's license
And a can of oil to bribe the joints
of an old combine into one more season

ELLARAINE LOCKIE

Those Montana Men

His name is Roy
and he calls me Babe
Born and bred Montanan
Like all the men
who mesmerize me
With silver belt buckles
big enough to bring down steers
And shit-kicking cowboy boots
shined for Saturday night dances
where men two-step
instead of two-time
Rough and ready in public
Tender and ready in private
Gutsy guys who rodeo ride
but breech-birth calves
Garth Brooks' kind of caring
Cool pool and bar beers
don't cancel 5:00 a.m. chores
defeat 14-hour work days
Or curb appetites for country
cooking and long loving
The real McCoys
Except for Roy
Who isn't a real Roy
His mom named him Noël
But he makes me feel
like a real Babe

ELLARAINE LOCKIE

Rebellion

Stay away from amusement park rides
country roads and horses said the neurologist
after the rupture of a disc
Could have been my father dictating
that rivers, convertibles and horses
were too dangerous for his only daughter
Who had to pretend with a stick horse named Trigger

In middle age I have blossomed
in the fiery glow of rebellion
The embers fall like petals surrounding Sadie
Me in neck brace and cowboy boots
She the bridge connecting me
to hallowed ground of my family homestead

Reason says the oatcakes I've fed her every summer
account for the whole-heart gift
of submission she grants me
Instinct says she knows age and hard times
had her headed for the dog food factory
And that we were related long before I adopted her
That our ancestors have entwined for generations

Back at the barn the last foal she'll ever have whinnies
She answers a comfort but another call too
From the open range, clover and wild grasses
We continue her easy gait
Heedless to a red-tailed hawk's scream
as he circles a prairie dog hole

Below hooves crunch rattlepod
Pound smells of sage, dropseed and manure
out of the soil our grandparents toiled
Sustenance we breathe in as we move
toward the flames of sunset in front of us
Like sisters following the same trail
Manes flying free in the prairie breeze

ADAM TAVEL

Letter to Weingarten Written as the Script
for an Imaginary Western

Fade in: an ochre dusk hovers
over the Sierra Madres. A mouthful
of chewed black licorice serves
as venom you've sucked from the pasty
flab of my thigh. Spitting

the dark spume at menorahs
of clustered cacti prickling
a deflated orange balloon of sun,
you recite your favorite Longfellow
as we saunter the lonesome mile
back to Blueberry Gulch, a brothel

penned by a mining town. My third
rattler bite in a week, you christen me
Fat Freddy Fang-Fucked while I curse
the inky lips upon your face, ordaining
you the worst protagonist this side

of Saturn. None of our banter furthers
the plot. The plot revolves
around your impending showdown
with Toothless Lars, a Norwegian prick.
He sweats gin and smokes his Colts
at the Kiowa squaw who hangs

starched Franciscan linens on a line
behind the old mission. There, dust
makes a soundless ballad riding
the dew-dawn breeze that dies
just as the friar's ward of orphans

rasps their colic. Jumpcut: these angels
will blast your nads to smithereens
you roar, wiping a belt
of whiskey from your lips before
drawing both six-guns. Gut-shot,
you find the strength to plug

Lars so full of lead I can't count
the legion names for light
streaming through his ribs
as you slump into the dust. One cello
bellows its legato question mark
before I gimp a-weeping

to your side. If you can bless a field
of heather in Ohio, you croak, bury
my whiskers there, but lickety-split I roll
my sidekick sleeves and bowie the bullet
from your belly. Heal thyself, I say,

it's a nine o'clock curtain for Gimpy
Bess who twirls her nude bolero.
We limp to stanchions swigging
a bottomless flask where
we slouch and toe the names

of flame-haired hosanna sweethearts
in the dust. I envy your Dean Martin
grin and sloppy Stetson brim.
You beg me not to hum
my off-pitch rendition of "Blood
on the Saddle." We waste

the final scene stoned
on peyote tying ribbons
in our Palomino's mane,
a beast we ride forever
into the scrolling credits.

KLIPSCHUTZ

The Hero with a Thousand Faces Rides Again

Kit Carson shook my hand on the California Zephyr outside Roseville.
Five nowheres later he detrained in utter darkness

> *Got to meet up with my mom.*

to press on through this hard-sell real estate, Kit behind the wheel,
Sioux City-bound, for a ninetieth birthday party, Labor Day.
(This side the grave, mom fears one human only.)

> *Hell yeah. It's a surprise!*

Kit whips out his wallet so I can see his license and a snapshot:
Grandmother Of Us All: a beaming specimen, white-helmeted,
outlaster of two husbands, she gardens, bakes, crochets and volunteers.

> *Same home since she was twenny.*

Kit offers me a Pepsi from his cooler. Sealed plexiglass absorbs
the dying light, petrochemical, reflective, closing in. A light tap on
my shoulder for the road (*Take it slow*) and a Gary Cooper screen kiss
for the gal from New Orleans been warming up to him since Winnemucca.

> *Elko must be out here somewhere.*

MICHELLE BONCZEK

Chico Hot Springs Saloon, MT

I'm tempted to call it
Yellowstone's crown, how it sits
above the park, just after

sharpened roadside cliffs and wild
mountain sheep nibbling grass, a rustic
resort where women—young women,

the regulars, in pretty clothes sit
at high tables waiting
for men in cowboy boots to lift

their hands and guide them
to the dance floor.
The live band plays country,

the singer wears a silver cowboy hat
while the bassist, you can tell, wants
nothing but to play jazz.

The couples circle each other's bodies,
step with the music. It is so easy
to make up the story. One man

in tight blue jeans, sandy hair falling
far below his neckline, has a hard groove
and no form. He's the type of dancer

my father used to say would pull
a girl's arm from her socket.
He's all hip and swing, untempered

patter of boots. His partners dizzy
yet come back song after song for another
spin. One man, the gentleman, slightly

older, is a perfect square. His shoulders,
his hips, he holds the waist of his partner
like a strong wind. He looks into her

eyes and she glides anywhere
his motion takes her. And among
the girls, the middle-aged woman,

you can tell, gorgeous once, still
slim and energetic, laughing
in a leopard skin-patterned shirt slipping

from her shoulder, claps her hands
to the music, slaps her thigh, dances alone
some songs, at the front of the floor.

DAVID LAVAR COY

Working Below Zero

The cows accept the weather.
They lie down, curl up,
and let the snow fall on their backs,
let it crystallize their ear hairs.

Around here leisure is hardship.

I fight rusty bolts with a wrench,
and scrape my bare knuckles.
I will be taking the project
indoors, into the tool shed,
starting a fire with matches
and a *Playboy* magazine
to thaw things out.

No progress without blood on your hands.

Soon, god willing, I'll haul bales,
bust them open and scatter hay
with a pitchfork. The cows can decide
whether to eat it or bed down in it,
while I go break the ice on their water.
With luck, the world will be warmer
tomorrow and I can keep my gloves on.

Uncertainty is a mother of contention.

David Lavar Coy

Horses and Cowboys Suffer Together

They smell our sweat
and buzz in
to harass us

those long black horseflies
whose bites
can make skin shutter.

We strip off saddles,
bridles, blankets,
release the horses—

every horse
for itself. Some stand
together, swat

in a rhythm,
positioned head to tail,
tail to head,

with teeth they
scratch each other's itches.
Some gallop in circles,

kicking up dust,
then lie down on their backs
and roll. As for us,

it's duck and dodge,
wave our hats
run in any direction

end up indoors. Outside
the sun shines on wild
yellow daisies.

LYLA D. HAMILTON

Trail Ride

Carpets of columbine at seven thousand feet.
Purple and white overshadow other blossoms.

Jimmy, a young wrangler
With a soft Texas accent,
Leads our small band through meadows
And aspen groves.

He already knows the horses
And the land.
He swiftly appraises the riders.

Sassy, the mare I ride, lives up to her name.
Snatches at shrubs as if she's hungry.

After months of carrying dudes on these trails
She knows when they'll gaze at the mountains
And not notice where her head is.

I delight in having a mount
With a little spirit.
I'd rather not
Be just a passenger.

My beloved older sister—
The one who can entice the child in me
To come out and play—
Rides Magnum,
A sluggish gelding.

I'm surprised
That she's chosen
To join me
For a trail ride.

She loves to dance in spangled frocks
The way I love to ride in jeans.

Yes, I recall a photo from our childhood:
We two ride double
On Star, the placid black mare
Who carried each of us
Of that generation and the next

As we explored and savored
The arid, rugged, splendid place
Our forbears homesteaded.

Citified now,
My sister finds the West's
Endless expanses
Alien.
Eerie.

She no longer
Recognizes animals
As familiars.

She doesn't realize
That Magnum can read her.
She couldn't foresee
That he would reveal her.

He knows the route.
Plods in the same direction
As the other horses
But chooses different branches of the trail.
Sets his own pace.

They fall behind.
My sister wails,
"He won't go where I tell him."

She complains to the universe.
"He takes his own path.
He doesn't follow the other horses."

Magnum realizes that
Someone must take charge.
Choose the path for them.
And that this rider
Doesn't know how.
A two-hour trail ride
Embodies
In miniature
Her life struggles.

I suddenly remember
That she never learned
To right herself

On ski slopes.
Always
Waited
Instead
For rescue.

I turn away
To hide my tears.

Jimmy gathers the stragglers
And calls back two riders
Who've ventured too far ahead.
He brings the herd together
To keep the riders safe.

Sassy flattens her ears.
Warns
Others in the string
To respect her space.

Her spacious space.

Something on the ground
Startles her.

She jumps.

Magnum
Wisely
Defers to Sassy.
Abruptly
Moves away.

My sister squeals.
Jimmy calms
Horse and rider.
Speaks quietly to my sister
Then clips a rope to Magnum's bridle.

And leads them home.

BRENDA YATES

Blood Brothers
for Nan Hoskins

Every Saturday at the matinee, a lone man
took action, saved a town or wagon train
then rode away into next week's episode.
He outdrew, outshot or outsmarted
outlaws, gunslingers, cattle thieves and crooks.
With few words, he dealt justice
to a corrupt sheriff, a greedy rancher,
put backbone into the drunken judge
or cowardly dry-goods merchant and became
blood brother to an Apache chief.
His horse understood him best.

But women always cried, even the tough ones
in the saloon. The weaker sex got all weepy
when captured and again when rescued or
were sure to take some notion that the cowboy
was more than just friends then be all misty-eyed
when he left. We knew: tears sapped strength.
They were bad water, worse than the salty spring
the cowboy warned against—give in,
just once, and you were doomed.

Lizzie and I made our pact:
took the sharpest knife from the kitchen drawer,
decided our knees would be best
since they were the most used to bleeding.
Lizzie still had the hard purple streaks
her bike'd gouged down her shin and my scabs
weren't healed from the fence last week.

We couldn't make
the determined slice we'd seen on screen,
so scraped a little at a time, fuzzy
white to naked pink, until the skin was raw
and seeping. We pressed knee to knee,
repeated solemn words we'd heard cowboys
use and then the secret ones they didn't say
out loud: We'll never cry, no matter what.

We wiped the knife, hid the red Kleenex
in the bottom of the trash and went outside
to wait for Momma to come back and drive us—
out to the stables for the riding lessons
we'd won at the matinee.
Like finding sweet water.
I imagine a pinto for you
and a gray for me.

ANNA MOORE

Simile

As in the election-night broadcast we all watched
when the wide-smiling cowboy senator
had to preside over the spectacle of his own defeat—
and despite the cameras, the white lights,
and his many years in politics,
he fixed his eyes on his cuff's pearled
buttons and stood silent, deaf
to the hollers and whoops
that ricocheted off the walls around him

so, my once-omnipotent father stood,
laid off from his fourth job in five years,
mute under the floodlights in our driveway—
eyes fixed on the grooved leather of his watch band,
the weekday brown of his shoes,
and the contractor's brand in the sidewalk,
while around him the October night filled
with bay leaves, television, and kitchen cabinets,
—and how long was it before he heard
his children shouting at him to come inside?

Carol Guerrero-Murphy

To Pray at the Altar of this Horse

You must scratch his withers
before you bend your neck
before you push your head into his shoulder.

You must brush the mud on his coat
with curry comb and bristles
for he rolls in puddles and ditches.
You must pick gorse out of his tail with apologies
for he prefers to sleep tangled in the bush when it's cold.
You must accept his hooves into your hands to pick them.
You must clean his sheath and foreskin respectfully.
You must teach yourself to be a handmaid
who wipes his eyes, strips gnats from his ear-linings,
massages his scars and checks his teeth and feet.
When you pray at his shoulder, you must accept
the odors of mouth and tail, must adore the smell of his skin.
When you pray, you must joyfully breathe
hair and dust into your mouth and be grateful.
After he is clean you must give him an offering—
oats or graham crackers or alfalfa hay.

You must revere the vet and the farier, his priests.

To pray at the altar of this horse
you must hope for good weather, for whether blizzard
or choking cloud of brown wind or painful sun
you must find him far out in a field and when you approach him
you must look down aside.
You must ring the bells of the halter buckles,
you must square your shoulders and stand strong
and never get under his feet without his knowing.

At the altar of this horse you may offer silent prayer or songs.
To pray at the altar of this horse you must humble yourself
and in serving this horse, consider it exaltation,
for he carries you above
cold rivers, sharp stones, and thistled grassland.

CAROL GUERRERO-MURPHY

Lucky Says

One: take this with you, this you cantering bareback, this you
I carry across the last green meadow of fall, take yourself
this way, and this meadow, and me, into every closed room,
take this outdoor you, carry yourself as I carry you, broadly, strong, indoors
and as I swerve dangerously out from under you, take yourself laughing,
hanging on as I jostle into a trot, take the one who threads her fingers
through my coarse mane, take the laughing one, almost falling off,
always holding on, crossing autumn's meadows, take this
you laughing into the rooms of winter.

Two: I'm in the pasture and oats will arrive one day when
you're through moving things, moving objects here and there, your
        daughter out
of the house, your son back to his plane with his luggage, yourselves in
all four directions, cars breaking, bolts and oil raining, carbon
shooting out your car's exhaust as you shuttle objects back and forth between
stores and dorm rooms, stores and your homes, meals onto and off tables,
candles got out and lit and burned and snuffed, all the while,
I'm waiting in the deep grass, eating, and one day you'll arrive
and you'll be carrying my oats.

Three: I'm not the source of this love that sparks
soft fireworks between your fingers and my coat. Love spills
out of your fingertips brushing mosquitoes, pulling gorse,
and scratching, scratching my hide. Love is in the lover, not so
much the beloved. I love equally my oats, meadow
grass, wet mud on hot days, the mare in the next field, and you
brushing out my winter coat until my wild stripes show.

RED SHUTTLEWORTH

More . . . Your Gunslinger Shadow Grows Amber

To observe (absorb?) the enduring dead . . .

(Mysterious Dave Mather dead and wormy
in an Oakland flophouse
suggests the late work of a civilized West . . .
and no mystery beyond a need-of-cleaning
pistol mentioned in the crumbly will.)

. . . you must allow yourself
to be a lone figure
{clouds like concrete pressing down}
breaking your interior (ceiling?) calling.

All that aged, rotted flophouse drywall
falling in chunks from the heaven of others.

Old pal Bat Masterson yet approaches
his squarish New York City journalist form.
Steak-clogged arteries.

These are primary juxtapositions:
Old West and walking pantomime.
What a goddamned trick:
levitation with the dead.

To the Memory of Ed Dorn

TRICIA KNOLL

Assisted Living in a Rocking Chair

Front to back roll, her mind knits
limp smells of a damp wool saddle blanket,
afghans, and fingerless mittens for knobby hands
with black felt hats for sun-scorched, sweaty heads.

Her eyelids droop; toes stretch, push and crack
open the smell of dusty mid-winter late afternoon.
She stumble-hums don't let girls grow
up like cowboys, knees bowed like spoons.

One lumpy red-plaid pillow massages
her bony butt, saddle burn, rocker canters
a mare named Paint or Patsy,
slow lope in a mountain meadow

with stiff leather gloves clutching oiled reins.
She and a paint quarter horse mare pick
an abandoned trail through stream bed rocks,
amble-passing a fastness of blue flax.

Solid horseflesh rubs her groin and thighs,
rawhide, warm, wet, and rolling rocker sighs.
Come sundown, she does not see with open eyes.

CAROLYN DAHL

Carrying Our Loads

Driving at night, my car a silent capsule pulled along the freeway's string,
big rigs with Great Dane snouts crawl up behind me, nudge the air, snort

at bumpers like chained bulls. Cat-eyed lights rake my car's packed
interior, reveal a single me, uneasy as a paper target at a shooting range.

The drivers in frayed cowboy hats or trim Stetsons, with old-god faces
dulled with the opium of miles, don't detour from their compass

of purpose. Wanderlust is their only desire. Neither smiling
nor frowning, they grumble truck gears, pull out, wobble

my small car with their long trailers of secrets outlined in lights
like rodeo carnival rides. The drivers are guardians of roundups

I can't see: apples, aliens, oil, calves, chemicals, or radioactive
uranium. Level with wheels, I watch the revolution of tires,

the rubber braille-bumps the roads thin to flung black
curls I mistake for fallen animals. Sometimes real ones rise

from the grass—hunted deer seeking safety in no-gun zones
who grow crazy with the consistency of headlights, leap

like saints into the promise of chrome. The drivers swerve,
but in the country music of night, no one stops for shadows,

or deer bounding into grass, though we glance in mirrors
that look back at all the shattered songs we leave behind.

CAROLYN DAHL

A Rancher's Rainstorm

We writers sit on his porch when the sky opens. Dog Bob, moved by lightning, drags his buckshot-filled butt to lay under the table across our damp and muddy-socked toes. Sid turns in his chair. "You can't cuss the rain, if you need it." He raises a jubilant fist to the sky, shakes it like a rain rattle, roaring. "Come on. Come on you storm."

His silver-haired profile sharpens against the wet screen sliding off the roof slats, cutting the landscape into slices like black rain lines in a Japanese woodcut.

"So writers, write about this storm," he shouts through cupped hands, out-hammering the thunder with his pounding voice. We pull our chins into jacket collars as the air on the porch grows cold as well water, so thick with moisture that a deep breath could feel like drowning. We write: *When it comes, it runs through ice cubes. The grass clumps tremble with the beating, while puddles jump and splash as if seeded with leaping tadpoles.*

We write through the moisture, force the curling pages down, watch the pine trees bend to the rain-dam breaking on their sap-filled boughs. Our inks grab the fibers of the paper, refusing to gray out, but hold the color like the dark pines of a Chinese painting.

"Damn you sucking junipers." He stamps his feet as if he could stop the roots' silent slurping. "Drink two hundred gallons a day. My rain," he shouts. We write: *The mud on the road goes slick as silk, sliding on itself down the hill. Scrubbed mud, rubbed mud, blending shards and arrowheads in water ridges, erasing tire tracks of pickup trucks and horses' feet.*

Sid stands. "That's the last kick of the horse," he says as the thunder subsides. "Hell of a ride." The sky, depleted and subdued, drips its last spots on our pads, smearing whatever we wrote. We blot the raindrops mixed with ink off on our jeans to join the dirt we carry in our hiking pockets, cuffs, and hair.

Sid, mood changed like the weather, steps off his porch of hand-hewn Ponderosa pine hitting the steps he built to reach the land sooner than a door can open, sniffs the air for bear, elk, beaten mint, the smell of satisfied soil under new sun.

Someone asks, "How much rain fell, Sid? Six inches?" Lost in his personal landscape, Sid never turns. "I don't measure the rain. I measure the grass."

LEONORE WILSON

The Cattle

*"And what about all the rest of the animality that's embedded so deeply
in our lives? What about the cattle that live so close to humans? What
about the herds of cows returning at dusk from their pastures, lifting their
tails and shitting in the middle of the village? What about the cattle smell,
which reminds us of where we really come from? When that disappears,
when it vanishes from our everyday existence, there'll be nothing left that
is capable of assuaging our loneliness."*—Andrzej Stasiuk, FADO[1]

To live among these bulwarks of silence with their fat-tongued
Watery chorus, their constant piss and shit and aimless butting and shoving
Is to know what buoys the long January tedium, what caulks the fog from
    seeping
Into the mind's bowl of glutted doubt where questions climb like toying
    branches
Asking what use is living after one's children have departed, after one's
    occupation
Has folded like the wings of a bat—dumb varmint blindly circling
The living room as if it could find any modicum of bliss.

                Without the pasture's beasts
I, a mother/wife would seep into a spell of a much crueler brooding,
For they have always kept me company, although at times
I shouted, brandishing a willow stick, driving them from the field
Where they had lingered like big-eyed relatives at the picture window
As the children lay napping, swaddled in their cradles; my herding necessary
In my lactating days when my hair remained unbraided, my bathrobe stained
With burped-up spittle, my brain rattled by the repetitive cries
That pinned me, a mad Prometheus, twisting in her own barbed-wire.
Then every outside noise bugled in my head,
Then every second a child slept was godly-quiet alchemy.

Then one day in glistening spring
When the twins and the baby were three and two respectively,
I walked out further, took the rutted half-mile trail to the neighbor's glade.
I shaped my irregular feet to the muddied-bovine prints as if to slow my pace,
To acquire fortitude and patience. Nearing the meadow's weathered gate
I saw the fresh-wet body of a bull calf shivering in streaks of blood,
Eyes clouded and dimmed in mucous; legs curled like maidenhairs
   beneath it.

And I crouched down, shuttled my palm beneath the rakish fur,
To feel its heart; oh I stayed there probably longer than I should,
Believing if abandoned it would surely die; I stroked its gut,
Rubbed its muzzle, but soon duty called and I hurried back
To my dozing trinity, only to meet the foreman on his pony,
Who when questioned told me how cows will often wander
Upon giving birth, that they need about an hour after labor
To harness their own strength, to nourish their own hunger;

        How this balm became my creed, my sleep—
That I was more like them than I believed, my browsing sister-kin;
Our flow-lines understood, a stalwart pushing through the hay.

[1]Andrzej Stasiuk, FADO (London: Dalkey Archive Press, 2009), 67.

JOHN McCARTHY

Ode to Robert McClure

Wearing the boots in school
got him the nickname.
Forty years of epilepsy
did not get him a real hire.
With a revolving squeegee,
steel handle stoic, he walks
to work walks to work walks
to work all in the same day.
Homeless, sun-sunken eyes,
callus hands—friendliest grip
of tragedy. He met Bobbie Jean
when she worked the Route 66
tourist attraction and he's been
faithful to her gravestone since.
Between Oakridge cemetery,
he retraces footsteps of Lincoln
through race riot ghost dust
and farewell addresses to wash
the windows of local businesses,
turning elbow grease for bags
of donuts and roses, giving
the red petals to Springfield
bar patrons and concrete strangers.
Transparency in business is good;
if customers can't look inside,
they will not bother to make
expectations, so erase the smudge.
A few bucks later when you can see,
Cowboy vanishes.

GINA BERNARD

Raw

April snow disregards the carcass,
which has wrestled to the surface
despite ignorant drifts unaware
they conceal its position near the fence.

She reins her horse, contemplating
the spindrift coil and whorl—a high plains
calligraphy of spring—as it writes
across bone in its fine cursive hand.

Nothing stays buried long, she concedes
and leads the mare from where a scapula
blade spreads itself like a gray and ugly
rumor. An angry scrim of iron sky

spits at her face, pulled taut beneath
the brim of a Stetson. She shifts
in the saddle, leather grimacing
beneath time-worn denim. Her crossing

has taken years—passages marked
by cairns of blood and broken bone.
The too-familiar gazes from emergency
room nurses who would not meet her eye.

December had witnessed his last raised
voice. And hand. Wyoming raged with the first
of winter's storms. The world ground to a halt
and laid its shoulder to the solstice.

He had tried to tame her, she supposes,
his love cruel and unyielding. No matter now.
Come spring, a shovel will testify
the accusations her pistol had finally leveled.

DON THACKREY

After Chores

When chores are done and all the livestock fed,
Before I kneel for prayer beside the bed,
I'll take a bit of time to meditate
On what needs done tomorrow, what can wait,
And in this way I slowly get ahead.

Upon this several-thousand-acre spread
And herd of Angus cattle, hundred head,
I've built a life I can appreciate
              When chores are done.

The grassland greening up, the heifers bred,
I should be breathing easy, but instead,
I find I'm melancholy with a freight
Of thought about what future may await
A restless rancher once his God has said,
              "Your chores are done."

Cowboys

They didn't look like rodeo cowboys should.
The bronc rider, Kevin,
could pass for a small-town running back
in work boots and muscle shirts.
Les, the short one, rode the bulls,
but dressed in overalls
and a wide straw hat at work.
At Friday quitting time they drove all night
to rodeos, Mondays pulled in straight from the road.

They planned to ride in every town they could
on the long July Fourth weekend,
but only Kevin came back.
Les was laid up in Amarillo
where the bull had broken his leg in three places.
But that won't make him give up rodeo.
Kevin points out his own scars,
a hospital tour of the southern plains—
pins in one leg at Lubbock,
three cracked ribs in Carlsbad,
collarbone screwed together in Wichita Falls.

They both grew up near Bottomless Lakes,
where early cowboys tied rocks to their ropes
and fed them in, but never found the bottom.
Legend had it someone drowned at the lakes
and washed up in a cavern fifty miles south.
Nothing in that border country is constant,
Ciudad Juarez and the Rio Grande
just hours away, intermittent streams,

irrigated hay the only green for days,
another world moving under the sand.
They learned to travel fast and light,
ready to run wide-open, to fix the rope
and brace against the animal's torque.

WILLIAM NOTTER

The Ranch Woman's Secret

Arlan thinks I'm here to watch the sunset
the days he finds me still outside on the deck.
It would likely be grounds for divorce if he knew,
but I'm here listening for coyotes who cry in the hills
when the sun is gone and twilight purples the east.
I do the books, and I know he's wasted more
on traps and shells and bait than we've ever lost
to coyotes. We haven't had a single head
killed by anything but cold and blizzards
or the scours in years. I know it's the bank note
and the markets he mumbles about while he sleeps,
but it's coyotes in the morning. He can't sit still
thinking of all the space they've got to hide in.
And the harder he fights to run them out,
the more I hear wailing in the hills at night.
We saw one crossing the road one evening, her coat
like ruffled wheat, looking back at us
as if we were out of place. Arlan stopped
the truck and shot her with his coyote rifle.
She spun once, biting the wound, then dropped,
and he hung her carcass on the barbed wire fence.
I fell asleep on the couch every night that week,
but he never knew why. He'll start to wonder
where he put his seven-millimeter shells
and how his traps get sprung while he's in town
or hauling a load of hay from Nebraska. The coyotes
won't let him win, and I'll keep staying out
past dark to listen, to hear the anxious cries
that make these nights, this stubborn life, seem real.

F. Brett Cox

First Rodeo

A different sky in Colorado
Puffs of cloud so sharp and motionless
It's like you're seeing them through 3-D glasses

The barrel race is
The easiest thing to watch

Bull riding is insane
Calf roping is just sad
Don't get me started on bucking broncos

But the races where these women charge out
And loop their horses around the barrels
Lean impossibly as they make their turns
One right after the other
Now that's beautiful

Especially tonight when the wreck on the interstate
Backs up the traffic for over an hour
And they run some extra races

With the music turned off
And the crowd thinned out
You can hear the horses gallop
Hear the hooves hit the dirt
Hear what the riders hear

Afterward they probably go to a bar
Drink their beers
Probably talk of the ride tonight
Maybe the next one tomorrow

But there's no telling really
The only certainty is

The sky is not different for them
The clouds are clouds

Tom Sheehan

Burial for Horsemen

(For my father, blind too early.)

The night we listened to Cochise's life
on records, and shadows remembered
their routes up the railed stairway like
a canyon's presence, I stood at your bed

counting the days you had conquered.
The bottlecap moon clattered into your
room in vagrant pieces . . . jagged blades
needing a strop or wheel for stabbing,

great spearhead chips pale in falling,
necks of smashed jars rasbora bright,
thin flaked edges tossing off the sun.
Under burden of the dread collection,

you sighed and turned in quilted repose
and rolled your hand in mine, searching
for lighting only found in your memory.
In moon's toss I saw the network of your

brain struggling for my face the way you
last saw it, a piece of light falling under
the hooves of a thousand Indian ponies,

night campsites riding upward in flames,
the prairie skyline coming legendary again.

DONNA KAZ

Big Horn Passover

Instead of lamb I eat Angus steer medium rare drenched in Heinz 57,
play pool with the only other customer while the jukebox
blasts a song about blue, and that's when he comes in
holding the local paper out in front of him like it was a matzo.

Mud spattered on his black hat, cattle dung caked on the heels of his boots,
gold buckle guarding the flat of his stomach, and except for the circle cut
made by the tin of Skoal in his right front pocket, his Wrangler rodeo jeans
    fit smooth
like they were poured from a mold of his waist on down.

He curves against the bar and leans left chewing on his paschal side of beef,
I know this night will be different from all other nights
as he eats without a sound, not even a faint scrape of the fork against
    the plate,
leaving nothing, his appetite huge and endless.

Suddenly he saunters (yes, I now know that I have never seen anyone
    saunter before)
and with outstretched arm his mighty hand tucks two quarters under
the lip of felt on the table. On all other nights I drink twelve-dollar glasses
of cheap red wine passing for Merlot in pretentious Soho bars

but on this night I drink Red Dog beer from the bottle in the oldest bar
    in Wyoming.
The game slows as winning is overshadowed by the tingling thrill
    of the chance
to play the cowboy. Counting the five solids I've left stranded I'm thinking
    my luck is cursed
when my partner calls the corner pocket and scratches out.

Without a blink the cowboy is racking up
saying, "I'd like to play partners. You and me
'gainst the bartender and the loser." He sidles towards me
(never saw anyone sidle either) sticks his hand out.

I grab what feels like grade 10 sandpaper,
his grip a saw dust massage, scream my name in his ear over the music,
pick up my stick, swallow hard, taste the bitter marinade
the steak has left on my tongue and bank a clean shot.

The angel of death hovers overhead and then passes.
A pack of cattle moves down the street outside,
the cowboy smiles and the distance between my house and his
falls together like the Red Sea.

RICK KEMPA

Long After Memory Is Gone

Long after memory is gone
he remains in an armchair in the parlor,
an old scarf wrapped around his neck.
With watery, droopy eyes he examines
the photo album on his lap,
a finger crooked above a face.
"Who's this? I don't believe I know this fella."
Grandma comes up behind him, yells in his ear.
"That's Ralph, your son-in-law, Blanche's husband."
He touches the photo for the connection.
"Oh yeah, yeah, I know him."

This is your great granddaughter Claire.
This is Fern, her mother. Here is your first son Tom.
His finger, a divining rod, moves upon the pages
then hovers, twitching in one spot.
Into his eyes a blue clarity comes.
"That's Fritz, by god! That's Fritz!
She was a good old mare!"

An April morning, a brisk wind at his back,
his thighs clinging to the warmth of her body,
the familiar heave beneath him as she mounts
the ridge behind the house. The sage,
stirred awake by their passage, envelops them.
Nostrils flare. "Best thing about her is
I don't have to tell her to face forward.
Not like some horses." He holds to the photo
as to her reins.

All day and then some he will ride her.
The warmth of her work will fill him
and he'll shed his scarf, finger the buttons
on his vest, every so often adjust his hat.
For the thousandth time supper will
grow old at the table.

HEATHER FOWLER

Sonnets of Selecting an Appaloosa

I

Under her black boot, the scent of grass, clover, dew,
Memories of the last thoroughbred who spooked too soon—
The rider watches the flanks, the horses' airs, moods.
If ever a poor time for bad selection, now.

New mounts must be willing to take a fence in stride,
Not shy away from sudden riverbeds or plunge,
Respond with pleasure when carrots are extended.
(For riders are partners in dangers together.)

She regrets her last was invisibly broken,
Lost, broken wrong, broken hard, broken mean, cracked steed.
The new will differ. Saddle? He'll not have seen this
'Til she arrives, leather in hand—reined in only

After bareback trials. For the moment, she watches,
Breathes, prays, intent on the high held head, far afield.

II

At times during training, a small rider must pause,
The strong buck of her horse near maniacal,
The whites of his rolling eyes, malice in his lunge.
She must remember, too: Who will be broken?

Why? Control all feats come after—when a woman
Seats the wide back of more powerful animals,
Fifteen hands high, makes them jump and sweat, leads from rings
To barn's rests, releasing tight straps, cleaning full hooves,

Digging with prongs to free nailed shoes from mud's debris,
Brushing the moisture and damp dust from stained bodies,
Praising their speed and found grace, praising their every
New willingness to please. Her glad face should nuzzle

Equine neck, show she is not a fly abuzz near.
Stand at left, between mount and walls—fearless, breed bonds.

III
That which is broken correctly does not feel harmed.
This is the first lesson in horse training. Watch close:
He who has been gentled can be better managed.
No broken spirit stands firm in the times of war.

Under her black boot, the scent of grass, clover, dew.
How beautiful the Appaloosa herd. She came
To see what the Nez Pierce once trained, to purchase this.
Memories of the last thoroughbred who spooked too soon

Still evoked how she'd had to put him down—yet, here, now,
The new will differ. Saddle? He'll not have seen this.
A few spot leopard with strong runs, she picks stallion
On the basis of how willing he is at heart.

If ever a poor time for bad selection, now.
For in her owning him, at ride, he owns her, too.

SALLY CLARK

Three Haiku

Haiku #1

my cowboy saddles
up his tractor, rides the range
corralling hay

Haiku #2

buffaloes at rest
in a sea of sandy wheat
boulders in the waves

Haiku #3

cows two-step in tall
grass, step and sway, tails swishing
out country rhythm

M.R. SMITH

Prayers for the World

In this late summer of my disgust
I leave the cottonwood bottomland for the higher
sagebrush ground creeping with cheat.

I work my horse down the fence line set with dropsy posts
and drooping rusted wire. I send up prayers
for the world and watch them scatter like quail.

At dusk we kick up sparks on stone,
as though forging iron nails upon earth's ancient anvil,
metalwork for vital repairs.

Bats come out against the blue-black horizon,
bruising that is difficult to watch while it quits the sky
and wounds the darkening homeward hills.

FICTION

MICHAEL SHAY

Cowboy Stories

Robert Wills was five beers into a Cheyenne Friday night as he told his favorite story to a middle-aged couple from Cincinnati.

"Buddies used to introduce me as Bob Wills, and the women would say 'You must be a Texas Playboy,' and I'd say that I wasn't any kind of Texan—I'm from Wyoming!" He cackled and tried not to trigger the cough that could go on and on and interfere with talking and drinking. He swallowed the last of the cheap draft and slapped the empty beer glass on the bar's soggy coaster. He rocked the glass, hoping that these tourists would notice his thirsty state and spring for another round.

"Who's Bob Wills?" The woman exhaled a stream of smoke and then waved it away with a sweep of her flabby arm.

Robert noticed her long lashes and blue eyes. They belonged to a face that was once pretty but now was creased with lines and droopy at the jaw line.

"You never heard of Bob Wills and his Texas Playboys?" Bob asked.

The woman's husband raised his glass. "Here's to Bob Wills and Texas Swing."

He took a long draw on the beer. "Great stuff."

Robert didn't know if he meant the music or the beer. "Damn straight," he said, an all-purpose reply.

"Well, hon," said the woman, eyes on her husband, "I don't know who they are. Should I?"

He nodded his big head. "Saw 'em once down in Lubbock." He looked over at his wife. "I was in the Army—before I met you. That band played some good dancin' music."

"You don't dance with me," she said.

"Bob Wills is dead."

"But you ain't." A pout added more wrinkles to her face.

"I'll drink to that." Robert raised his empty glass. The man and woman raised theirs. Robert was hoping that they would notice his sad state of affairs and order up another round. Not a nickel to his name until his disability check came in next week—*late* next week.

The man put his half-finished glass on the bar. "We gotta go." The woman put her glass next to his.

"Got a smoke?" Robert asked the tourist woman. She hesitated briefly, and then tapped a cigarette out of the pack and handed it to Robert. It was a long thin cigarette with a pink filter. "Fancy," he said, balancing it on his lip. He pulled out his old Zippo and lit up. He tasted more mint than smoke.

"That's not going to blow up, is it?" She pointed at the oxygen canister in a sling at Robert's side.

"Hasn't yet."

Her husband laughed. "First time for everything."

Oxygen bottles don't blow up, he wanted to say. It still felt a little strange to wear this wheezing contraption around town. It was better than those big canisters that he used to wheel up and down city streets. People would just stop and stare at this little cowboy, couldn't be more than five feet tall, as he hauled around a big green thing that looked like a submarine torpedo—that's how one of the guys at the Legion Hall had described it. Long plastic hose snaked out of it into his nose, a nuisance at first but now something he had to live with.

"Maureen, I'd say it's time to go." The man eased off of his stool and tossed some bills on the bar.

"Pleased to meet you." Maureen nodded at Robert and grabbed a purse the size of a shopping bag.

Robert touched the brim of his cowboy hat. "Ma'am."

The couple was three steps to the door when Robert grabbed their beer glasses and dragged them over to his spot. The glasses were still cool to the touch. Jack the one-eyed bartender was busy at the far end so Robert emptied the glasses into his, sloshing some on the counter. He sipped, slowly, and wondered if any other tourists would happen by tonight.

Jack walked over, picked up the empty glasses. "You scaring away my customers?" His black beard matched the patch on his left eye.

"C'mon, Jack, you know better than that." Robert smiled and drank his beer. "I'm the only gen-yu-wine cowboy in this place."

"Gen-yu-wine pain in the ass."

"Just entertainin' the summer tourists," said Robert. "They want some Old West and I give it to 'em."

"Emphasis on *old*." Jack wiped down the bar. As he went, he grabbed tips and stuffed them into a huge mug next to the cash register.

"You should pay me to sit here and entertain your customers."

"How about I pay you to stay away?"

"How much?"

Jack grinned, teeth white as a cloud against his beard. "I'll pay you twenty bucks if you never come in again."

Robert's eyes brightened. "Really?"

"There's a catch." Jack leaned across the bar. "You have to collect in person."

"But if I come in . . . "

"You can't make twenty bucks." Jack barked a laugh as he pushed himself away. "That's the catch."

Robert shook his head. "Not much of a deal." That's the way it was, always a catch. He had no money because he cowboyed for peanuts all of his life and what he did make he pissed away. He got disability for his asbestosis and emphysema but didn't get diddly from Social Security because most of his employers had paid him under the table. If it weren't for free care at the Cheyenne VA Hospital he'd be in real trouble. Those four years in the Navy in the 'tween years—between Korea and Vietnam—had been worth it. But he suspected it was the exposure to asbestos on that old rust bucket, the USS Egan P. Dooley, which had ruined his lungs. He had clambered to join a class action suit by other veterans but didn't qualify for some reason he still didn't understand.

"These seats taken?" A young guy in jeans and a flowered Western shirt smiled. Next to him was a tall guy with spiky blonde hair dusted black at the tips. He was dressed all in black.

"Be my guest," said Robert.

"Thanks," said the first man. "I'm Jonathan Rhiems and my friend's name is Christian."

"How-dee!" Christian said with the over-exaggeration of a non-English speaker.

"Where you from?" Robert asked.

"Sweden," said Christian.

"L.A.," said Jonathan. "What are you drinking?"

"Draft," Robert said eagerly. "Better make it a tall one."

Jack came over and tossed dry coasters on the bar. He shot Robert his Cyclops evil eye. The new guys ordered bottles of beer. Robert didn't catch the name. The bottles arrived with colorful stylized rock formations on the labels.

"How do you say this?" Christian held up his bottle.

Robert read. "Vedauwoo Granite Ale. We say it Vee-duh-voo. They're rock formations between here and Laramie. I used to chase cows near there."

Christian said it slowly: "Vee-duh-voo."

"You speak good English," said Robert.

Christian shrugged. "I speak five languages."

"Here's to Sweden." Jonathan raised his bottle.

"Sweden," echoed Robert, raising his tall cold glass.

Christian rattled off a foreign phrase. "That's a Swedish toast to your continued good health," he explained.

They again raised their glasses. "Here's to mud in your eye," said Robert.

The men drank quickly and Robert kept up. Jonathan ordered another round. It always helped to be in the right place at the right time. Robert learned that the men were cinematographers making a movie about "The New West," whatever that was. They had already been to the Pine Ridge Reservation, Mount Rushmore and Montana's Big Horn Battlefield (Custer's Last Stand, thought Robert). They planned on filming some rodeos around Wyoming once the season heated up.

"Our goal is to juxtapose incongruous elements within the Western landscape," said Jonathan.

"Juxta-what?" asked Robert.

Jonathan sipped his fancy beer, obviously thinking about something. "Here's an example," he said finally. "We got four Indian guys from the Lakota nation to go with us to Mount Rushmore. They wore traditional garb. We posed them at various locations around the park, just like the four big heads on the mountain. One of them held a sign that read, 'The Black Hills Are Not for Sale.' The whites stole the place from the Indians, you know."

"It's not that simple," said Robert.

"I know—nothing ever is. But we're looking from some reaction, right?" Jonathan drank his beer. "Finally the rangers kicked us out, said we were making a nuisance. Must have been the fight."

"We have some great footage," Christian said. "Very real, very in-your-face filmmaking."

"Couple cowboys came along," continued Jonathan. "Thought we were making fun of the presidents."

"They thought I was a German," said Christian, waving around his beer. "They called me a Kraut. They said that us Krauts should get out of their park. That's stupid, calling a Swede a Kraut."

"So you busted the guy in the nose?" asked Robert. He'd been in a few fights and knew what to do: hit first, ask questions later.

"One of them tried to seize my camera. I just kept filming and Jonathan jumped on the man's back. The other cowboy got into it, and then along came a big park ranger who waded into the fracas."

"Where were the Indians?"

Jonathan laughed. "They sat on the rock and watched. Just looked on the whole time. When I asked them about it later, they just said it wasn't their fight."

"I was filming the whole time, even when the rangers kicked us out. That's rule number one—keep the camera rolling. You know what the rangers said. We didn't have a permit to film in the national park. Now that sounds like Germany—a permit for everything."

"What's the name of this movie?" asked Robert.

"Working title is *Real Indians and Real Cowboys*," said Jonathan.

"I'm a real cowboy."

The two filmmakers stared at the small man and his oxygen tank.

"Really?" asked Jonathan.

"Really." Before they could stop him, Robert launched into his history. Real cowboying in real places: Powder River Country in northern Wyoming, Cheyenne-area ranches, Colorado's North Park near Kremmling, and a decade in Arizona, some years spent at real ranches and some at a fake tourist trap. "I rode a horse before I could walk," he said. "At branding time, popped the nuts off many a calf."

"Popped nuts?" Christian stared.

Robert told them how he wielded a sharp pocket knife. "Got to pull each nut, then slice. Takes a practiced hand."

"Isn't it painful?" Christian's eyes were wide.

"They bawl plenty but it's over in a flash. You make sure they're not going to bleed out, then they're up and off to their mamas." Robert looked at Jonathan. "Hey Jon, how about another beer?"

"Sure—and please call me Jonathan."

While waiting for a refill, Robert hauled himself and his gear to the restroom.

When he returned, the men were in deep conversation. He sat back on his stool and started in on his new beer. Robert tried not to notice but Christian looked over at him several times, as if sizing him up for something.

By the time Jack hollered last call, the roving filmmakers had invited Robert to be part of their movie. All Robert had to do was pop some nuts on a calf and they would pay him two hundred dollars, as long as he signed a release.

"That's all fine and dandy," Robert said, "but nuttin' season is over."

"Over?"

Robert nodded. "It's June and the calves come in during May mostly." He sipped his beer and thought. "The Double Bar-V might have some late calves. I'll call the foreman out there."

"We'll pay him, too," said Christian.

After sealing the deal, they drove Robert home in their rented black SUV. He noticed all the bags and metal cases in the cargo area. They seemed like the real deal. Now he had to find some calves. Wouldn't be easy this late in the season. He had to admit that the money was good. They stopped in front of his apartment building.

"Pick me up here tomorrow at nine," said Robert as he got out of the SUV.

"Okay," said Christian.

As Robert went inside and waited for the elevator to his subsidized apartment in this old hotel, he felt vital again, knowing that he had a little unexpected money coming in. He called his pal at the Double Bar-V. Woke him up. Yeah, he had some late calves. Sure, he'd bring them in tomorrow if there was money in it. He liked the idea of being in a movie, said it would be good publicity for the ranch now that it was part of the local dude tour for tourists from Germany and China.

Robert sat back in his lone kitchen chair. He was going to be in the movies. Wait until the guys down at the bar heard about this.

* * *

"True story—I was in a movie." Robert sat at the bar. He drank a whiskey shot and beer.

"How did you get in a movie?" The guy at the bar wore a red-checkered shirt and gripped his whiskey with two meaty hands. The two guys next to him were dressed similarly. Easy to tell it was October and hunting season.

"It's called *Real Cowboys and Real Indians*—it's not out yet, and I only have a small part."

The man swiveled on his stool and looked at Robert. He sipped from his glass, taking in the worn cowboy duds and the oxygen bottle. "What kind of movie is it?"

The man looked semi-interested so Robert plunged ahead. "Documentary about the New West. Director is this guy from L.A., Jonathan-something, and Christian, the cameraman from Sweden. They wanted to see a branding and I took them out to one at the Double Bar-V."

"I've never been to a branding," the man said. He turned to his friends. "You?"

"When I was a kid," said the middle one. He wore a khaki cap from Cabela's. "My uncle had a ranch in the Sandhills. We used to drive out from Omaha."

"Not me," said the other. He gripped a Bud bottle. "Closest I've ever been to cows is the steak I plan on eating in a few minutes."

They all laughed.

Robert plunged ahead. "Foreman at the ranch—he's an old friend—had some late calves to brand so I took the movie guys out there. Just about forty minutes north of here. There was a girl along too. Jonathan said she was Pita and I said, 'Nice to meet you, Pita,' and she said that wasn't her name but she was with PETA—People for the Ethical Treatment of Animals. Some sort of anti-cow group."

"Enviros!" said the Bud bottle guy. "They hate meat-eaters."

"What was she doing there?" asked the guy in the cap.

"That was the weird part," said Robert. "She was thin as a rail, dressed in a jogging outfit. Quiet and serious. Anyway, we got to the ranch and the foreman teamed me and Jonathan up with this young Mexican cowboy. Christian was a few feet away with the camera and the girl. Cowboys thought his spiky hair was pretty funny.

"Anyway, the wrangler ropes the calf and Jonathan and I and the Mexican hold down the calf. He's bawling 'OwwwOwww,' that's what it sounds like, anyhow, calves calling to their mamas on the other side of the corral." Robert paused for a sip of his beer.

"I get out my knife—I always carry it." Robert lifted the scabbard with his right hand so the men could see it. "You get your knife, and the fur cover of the calf's balls, and then you squeeze. Out pops the bloody gray nuts. I slice each bloody sac and squeeze, cut one, toss it on the ground, and then cut the second."

"Rocky Mountain oysters," said the red-shirt man. "I've had those a few times."

"Right, but we don't take the time to put 'em in a bucket to keep the dirt off. We're popping and slicing." Robert paused. He was knee-deep in the story now and felt a cough coming on. Those coughing jags could last for a while and he didn't want to lose his audience. He held up his hand and swallowed some beer. The men were quiet.

"How you gentlemen doing?" asked one-eyed Jack from behind the bar. The three men asked for refills.

"And set up our friend here," said red-shirt guy, pointing at Robert.

"Much obliged," said Robert, evil eye glinting.

The round of drinks arrived.

"To Rocky Mountain oysters!" The man at the end of the bar held up his beer bottle. They all joined the toast.

"Bottom's up," said the man in the cap.

"All hell breaks loose," said Robert. "And it was my fault."

"How's that?"

"Couple things happened all at once. First of all, the girl from PETA has taken off her clothes and is naked as a jaybird behind me."

"No shit." This came from Jack, who stuck around after delivering the drinks.

"No shit. But I don't see her because I've taken the nut in my hand and I'm looking at it. I know the camera is recording all of this. I figure that it's time to give the movie a real down-home touch, a real look into cowboy culture. So I pop the nut into my mouth. Jonathan is watching me. His eyes get real big. He turns green. He barfs right on my jeans. Meanwhile, the Mexican's eyes are real big too, but that's because he's taking in the pale naked body of PETA girl. Not too many naked girls show up to brandings. I want to get away from Jonathan and wonder what the Mexican guy's looking at. So I turn, nut in mouth, and see a lily-white ass staring me in the face. It was a nice ass, I have to tell you, nicer than I would have thought, she being so skinny and all."

Everybody stared at Robert.

"The problem is, our attention is no longer on the calf. The calf wants none of this. He shakes off the Mexican, gets up in a burst of dust and runs past me to get to his mama. I hear a scream and I see the calf ram the girl and she falls bare-ass-over-teakettle—she's holding some sort of sign, too, but I can't read what it says. The sign flies up into the air. She crashes into Christian who also falls. The calf is going *OwwwOwwwOwww* and there's some screaming and yelling. I still have the nut in my mouth and I just about choke on it before I can get it spit out in the dust." Robert chuckled. "It was a sight."

His audience stared.

Jack shook his head, grabbed empty glasses, and stalked away.

"Wow," said the guy in the red shirt.

"That's all going to be in the movie?" asked the guy in the cap.

"Weird," said the guy at the end of the bar.

Robert slaked his thirst before answering. "I haven't seen the movie—it's not out yet. But Christian and Jonathan were kind of pissed off at the whole thing. This was going to be some sort of slam against ranching and they're the ones who bit the dust. The cowboys laughed so hard. Even the Mexican kid grinned when it was all over. The camera got all of it, I guess."

"They have those *Jackass* movies, where a bunch of guys do stupid things," said the guy at the end of the bar. "Could be one of those movies."

"*America's Funniest Home Videos!*" That was the man in the red shirt. "I'd watch it."

"They don't do naked girls," said the guy in the cap. "They'd edit it out."

Robert shook his head. "Christian said they wanted very real and very in-your-face filmmaking."

"Very ass-in-your-face filmmaking," said the man in the cap. The men laughed.

The red-shirt man drained his whiskey and stood. "We better scoot," he said.

"Early risin' tomorrow and off to the hills."

The other men finished their drinks and stood.

"Before you go," said Robert. "You guys remember Bob Wills?"

They all shook their heads.

"My buddies used to introduce me as Bob Wills and the women would say, 'You must be a Texas Playboy.' I'd reply, 'Hell no—I'm from Wyoming!'" He laughed and before he could stop it the coughing took hold. He doubled over. The coughs came from a deep place.

"Can we help?" asked the man in the red shirt.

"It'll pass," said Jack at the bar. "It always does."

Red shirt touched Robert's shoulder as he passed. One of the other men said, "Thanks for the story."

The other said, "See ya, Bob."

"Call me *Robert*." Robert managed to squeeze out between coughs.

"Robert," the man said, correcting himself.

Fifteen minutes later, Robert was sitting alone at the bar. He lit up a cigarette from his store-bought pack. It was getting near the end of the month again and he'd be back to hand-rolled in a few days. Back in June, those filmmakers had been a bit steamed at the turn of events at the ranch but had paid Robert in advance and he had been happy with his luck.

He thought about the sign that the PETA girl had been holding before she was run over by the calf. The PETA girl held the battered placard in her hand as they drove away from the ranch that day back in June. *Calves go nuts for carnivore cowboys.* At the time, he'd asked the girl if that shouldn't read "nutless" instead of "nuts." The girl, raw strawberry scrape on her forehead, had just looked blankly at Robert. It had been a tough day on the vegetarians.

Robert looked up at Jack behind the bar. His arms were crossed on his big chest.

His lone eye peered at Robert.

"What?" Robert asked.

"Damn fine story, Robert," said Jack.

"Thanks," said Robert. "And this one's true."

Jack shook his head and laughed. "Thought they were all true."

Robert held the laughter in check lest he burst into coughs. "Mostly true."

Jack grabbed a clean beer glass and filled it. He shoved it across the bar at Robert. Jack grabbed a bourbon glass and trickled a couple inches of Jack into it. He held up the glass. "Here's to mostly true."

They drank. Jack finished, moved on down the bar, and started his closing cleanup ritual.

Robert contemplated his lot in life. The stream of hunters would dry up in another month or so. Then would come the holiday revelers and downtown workers in for happy hours and then once again it would be summer with all the tourists. He had enough stories from his seventy years to make it through the seasons. A Bob Wills' waltz danced through his memory. "Mexicali Rose," his favorite. It almost kept time with the steady beat of the oxygen that allowed him to keep coming back for more.

Real Cowboy

He's a muscular angle against the barn door's frame. His back and one leg are straight. His other leg is bent, boot heel pressed against wood. Though his eyes are in a wedge of shade beneath his hat, he squints across the pasture, the arena, and the pine forest rising on the mountain. He smokes his cigarette like breathing, not even a pause when he places it at his lips, and he's careful to flick the ashes into the dirt. His name is Lloyd. He arrived at this Colorado ranch a month ago, and, other than the Idaho license plate on his Chevy truck, that's all I know.

His profile ignites me. I catch myself staring, and I know Lloyd feels my eyes. I flush. I weave the red prongs of the apple-picker through the straw and empty the manure into the almost-full wheelbarrow blocking the stall's gate. Ibn Soldad, the million-dollar stallion who produced this poop, whinnies to the mares from the lunging ring. It's his favorite hour, the time when John strolls to the pasture, halters a mare, and brings her to him.

I roll the wheelbarrow out the barn door into the sun and smell blazing dirt. I've been doing this for a month, but I strain against the weight. I'm tall for fourteen, but new bra and all, I probably still weigh less than the wheelbarrow's load. John, who owns this ranch, gets a kick out of my determination. Last week, Andrea, his wife, gave me a belt with a platter-size silver buckle etched with flowers.

"For your hard work," she said. Even though it pokes my stomach when I bend, I wear it every day. It's not hard to be good around here. Andrea feeds me three meals a day, and her and John's moods are as constant as the sunrise, which I've seen a lot lately.

When I pass the lunging ring, Lloyd holds a halter rope with the white stallion roiling at the end. Mane and tail churn the air. John leads Cammy, a bay mare, hauled here all the way from Montana, toward the gate. It's like Lloyd holds a storm, and his velvet murmurs soothe lightning. I strain to feel his words over the squeaking wheelbarrow. I imagine them spoken to me. The tops of my thighs tingle. I clench the handles, hold my back rigid, and find strength in my legs.

The manure spreader is a buckboard wagon with a metal barrel across the back that sends shit flying over the pastures as it's pulled behind a truck. Last week, I learned to drive. This week, John says he'll teach me to tow the spreader. I shovel in the new poop, lifting it high over the side. Behind me, I hear nickering and squealing and the men speaking low.

"Don't look, Kate," I say. But I always do.

Ibn starts at the head, breathing hard and fast as he takes in the mare's scents, and moves, herky-jerky, to Cammy's rump. Her back legs are hobbled, and his pink dick hangs long as my arm. As if they all have an agreement, Lloyd slackens the rope, and Ibn rears up, front legs bent at the knees, his hooves against Cammy's flanks, and the men stand, feet wide and ready, to protect both animals from themselves. Lloyd reaches out and guides Ibn into Cammy. There's nothing more beautiful than a horse rearing, but this is different. Ibn thrusts. I feel watery.

The second time I saw them breed a mare, I closed my eyes and pretended I was blind. But there came a moment when they all grew deathly quiet, and it was worse than watching. Now, when I watch, I hear that silence even more, and it's louder every time.

The silence comes again. Lloyd steps back and shortens the rope, and as Ibn backs off, Lloyd pulls him away from Cammy. John releases her legs and pulls the mare forward, so the horses are safely apart. John strokes her neck.

"Good girl," he coos. He leads her from the ring.

Lloyd removes Ibn's halter, pats his shoulder, and looks up. As I turn back to the manure, my cheeks crackle.

* * *

"Ease off the clutch," John says.

I ease my left foot back while pressing the gas with my right. The old Ford lurches, so I feed it more gas. We move forward, and the spreader clunks behind.

"Good," John says and nods, his mouth in the upside-down smile that tugs the corners of his gray moustache. "Now take the corner wide. A trailer always rides to the inside."

I take the corner wide, and we bounce onto the double-track that leads to the pasture. Gears scrape as I shift into second. Ahead of us, Lloyd crosses the track, sitting Ibn's trot like it isn't even there. He nods toward us, and

John lifts off his baseball cap and gives it a single wave out the window. I've never seen anyone but John on the stallion. *Don't look,* I think, but my neck betrays me. I study Lloyd from the side, then the back as the truck rolls along. Andrea told me at breakfast that tomorrow, she and John are going to town for feed and worming paste, and I imagine Lloyd striding up to me during their absence, his gaze earnest and yearning, and taking me in his arms. When I finally look away, I realize John is smirking.

"Someday, Kate, you're going to have men falling all over you," he says.

I force down a bark of laughter and lean forward to concentrate on driving. I'm wearing a baseball cap with my ponytail threaded through the back, like usual, and I remember Dad saying, "Your sister's going to have all the looks, so you'd better learn some skills."

John's words come as a shock. He knows Dad. They used to be friends, which is how I got here for the summer. I just called John and asked if I could work for him. Dad was furious. But they talked and talked on the phone, and he let me come.

"Hey," John says and makes me look at him. His moustache is straight now. "I know life's been hard. You deserve better."

"How were you and Dad ever friends?"

"Your mother's leaving hardened him."

"He *made* her leave."

"I had my part in that. Your mother was . . . special."

The truck lurches before I realize my foot's off the gas. I concentrate on driving, but the double-track's a haze.

John shakes his head. "He wasn't always cruel, Kate." After a minute he adds, "And he let you come here."

"Because of *you.*"

"And you," John says.

I snort.

He studies me. "Think on it," he says and glances ahead. "Gate."

I mash on the brake, and his palms meet the dash. The truck's door groans as he climbs out. My ears burn from the blood in them. I look down where the seat was cracked and is repaired with glue in a neat line.

John clanks loose the chain, swings the gate open, and lets me drive through. As I wait for him to climb back in the cab, Lloyd and Ibn canter through pale yellow grass along the fence line. I gaze at them and wonder if my mother ever felt this fire for Dad. And if she came to regret it. The memory of her dark braid and slender hands are all I've got of her. John must know I wish *he* was my father and Andrea was my mother.

John walks up to the driver's side window and surprises me. I fix my eyes on the steering wheel.

"You've got it from here," he says. As he turns to stroll back to the barn, he gives two quick slaps against the Ford's side and says, "Atta girl."

I study his lanky, bowlegged stride in the side mirror. He knew Mom's face, knew my parents as lovers. I try to imagine him and my father as friends. However it happened back then, I'm glad.

I drive to the pasture's far side, get out, and ratchet open the lever on the spreader. I bump back and forth with shit rooster-tailing behind and John's words echoing in my head. I take a long look in the rearview. I have muddy green eyes, a straight nose. Nothing remarkable.

I'm shaking my head as I get out of the truck and see Lloyd and Ibn canter toward me. I'm shocked still, but my knees drift. Ibn is an accomplishment of nature, and Lloyd is an even match. His head is tilted forward, and his right hand is steady in front of his stomach while his left, on the reins, is relaxed. As they get closer, little puffs rise when the stallion's hooves meet dirt, and I think about rain but smell baked grass, distant pine, and manure. I hear saddle leather creaking, the stallion's rhythmic exhalations, and the powerful squeak that rises from Ibn's flanks.

Part of me expects him to ride right on by. Other than a nod, Lloyd's never said a word to me. But he stops. He dismounts, lifts the reins over Ibn's ears, and turns to me. I realize I haven't moved, that the Ford's door stands open.

"Kate," he says and nods. He squints across the mountains as Ibn chomps the bit.

Etched on his belt buckle is a bronc rider with *Snake River Stampede* arced across the top. Ibn whinnies at the mares in the next pasture, and their heads yank up from the grass.

I can't speak. I've never been this close to him alone. I have to look up a little and fire sears through me. His eyes are blue, I realize. I had it wrong.

"I wonder if you'd like to have lunch tomorrow," he says, and it's all I can do not to collapse against the Ford.

"Yeah," I say.

"The house. Noon."

"Okay."

He lifts the reins over Ibn's swiveling ears and mounts. I feel the muscles beneath his clothes and concentrate on breathing. He glances down at me, and his lips hold a trace of smile. His boot heel presses gently into Ibn's side, and he leans forward as they trot away. It takes me a while to move, but I don't care because I know he won't look back. What just happened settles from my ears to my mouth in a smile, to my neck in a blush. My nipples harden, and I bend at the waist 'til my belt buckle jabs me. I put my hand over my heart and feel pounding.

"Holy crap," I say.

As I haul the spreader back, I glance in the rearview again and again.

* * *

John and Andrea pull up by the barn as they're leaving, and Andrea gestures for me to come over.

"There's plenty of lunch in the fridge," she says, and she lifts her blonde eyebrows high.

Behind me, Lloyd lunges a visiting mare in the ring, and Andrea glances at him, then at me.

She bites one side of her lip, which I've seen her do when she worries. She catches herself and smiles. "We'll be back around three. Need anything?"

I shake my head.

Beyond her, John grins. He shifts the truck into first, and I watch the tailgate as they roll away.

"You should've told 'em, Kate," I mutter.

I turn and see Lloyd, leaned back slightly to offset the lunge-line, the mare trotting, content, in a circle around him. I study the contour up the back of his Wranglers into the small puff of his shirt, along his back, to his shoulders, and into his hat. The truck is a distant plume of dust as I head to the barn.

Lloyd has his jobs and I have mine, but the three times we pass, he stares at me, and despite my efforts, I blush. When he's not near, I know where he is, and I can feel his body. I wonder if this sensing a person without seeing him is love. I imagine Mom sensing Dad.

Later, I imagine Mom sensing John, Dad sensing them sensing each other. Even though this would have happened before John married Andrea, I don't like it. Instead, I picture Andrea from my first week here. She's flushed, curvy in a dress, and pointing at my dinner in the oven before heading out to celebrate her five-year anniversary.

By eleven-thirty, when I head to the house, anyone touching me would get scorched.

I take the fastest shower in history, brush out my hair, and when I open the drawer for clean underwear, I notice a little velvet box on my dresser. Inside is a silver necklace with a charm of a horse rearing. Underneath is a tiny heart cut from construction paper with FROM J-N-A written on it.

My hand covers my mouth as I settle on the bed. It's easier when people are mean, I think. I flop back, naked, and feel like crying for how I've lied by keeping quiet when I hear the screen door slam.

I get dressed like a tornado and start for the kitchen, but I stop and put on the necklace. My skin is tanned where the silver horse rests, and my plain neck turns beautiful. I touch it, sigh, and stroll to the kitchen.

Lloyd's hat hangs on a hook by the door, and he sits at the table. On it are cold fried chicken, potato salad, coleslaw, and fresh strawberries. He stands as I enter.

"Kate," he says and nods.

"Lloyd," I say.

He pulls out the chair beside him. I can barely walk. I sit down, and he slides the chair forward behind me.

Lloyd lives in the cabin out back, but its kitchen is spare, so he's here most mornings. Sometimes lunch. Rarely dinner. He's usually out nights, and I've listened to his truck roll in after midnight with the radio playing low.

His hand rests on the table in a loose fist. I've stared at it while we've eaten with John and Andrea and imagined its calluses moving along my stomach. That hand reaches for the chicken and holds up the platter. I take a piece I know I won't eat.

When Andrea and John are here, I keep my eyes off Lloyd. Now, they move up the arm of his clean, blue shirt to his shoulder, and finally up to his face. I work to keep my breathing even. I notice that he has pocks up his neck and across his cheeks. A scar runs along his jaw, and the corners of his eyes and mouth are lined. Where his hair is newly trimmed over his ear and into his sideburn, there's a thread of pale skin. I picture him in the barber chair and see he's older than I thought. His nights out grow darker. I hear murky bars and tinkling ice in highball glasses. I smell the perfume of dusky women with low-cut shirts. I suck in my breath.

My hands fall to my lap. I swallow hard. I'm fourteen, and this is a real cowboy.

I study the food on the table. It's too carefully prepared to be leftovers. Before us are two glasses of lemonade, one of which Lloyd lifts to his lips, and I watch his sharp, clean-shaven Adam's apple go up, then down. Lloyd never drinks lemonade; he drinks water, black coffee, and beer. I touch the necklace and picture Andrea worrying her lip as she prepared this food.

"You don't have to do this," I say.

Lloyd assesses me like I'm a horse puzzling him. I feel the weight of his eyes, and I sweat, even on my stomach. I bunch the napkin in my lap and consider setting it on the table and leaving. But I can't.

Finally, he shakes his head. "It's just lunch."

"Okay," I croak. I reach for the potato salad.

We don't talk, we just eat, but his body is hot and dangerous beside me, and I think, Dad was right: I'm plain. How could I have been so stupid?

When we finish, we clean up with no sound but the scoot of dishes, the clink of silverware, and the faucet. As I turn from the sink, our arms touch. Our eyes meet, and mine fill with tears, so I look down.

"Come here," he says as he pulls me into his arms. They feel just like I'd imagined, except all I do is rest my head against his chest. The pearl snap of his shirt presses into my cheek, his chest rises and falls, and his belt buckle brands my stomach, just above my own. He smells like cigarettes and leather, and I wet his shirt with my tears. The dangerous part of me heats up, but he pulls back. He takes my cheek in his hand and runs his thumb along my jaw.

He leans down and kisses me, just in front of my ear, then on my jawbone.

"John's right. You're something *special*," he says with a trace of a smile, and he's at the door, reaching for his hat and stepping out in one motion. The screen door claps.

The ghost of his lips holds me still. His words unravel me, and I steady myself against the counter. I wobble to the porch and lean on the rail. My bones kindle as I watch Lloyd disappear into the barn, sense him setting to work. I press the stallion charm between my fingers and saw it back and forth along the chain. I feel the bump of each link against my neck.

PETER CLARKE

The Society Of Pardners To Melt Alaska

The third of January, 1959, was a cowboy's curse of a bad day for Texas. From the Oklahoma border to Cameron County and the tip of the Rio Grande, pardners awoke having to sober up to their first day of being "second biggest." Alaska had joined the Union.

No longer being the biggest, how was Texas to carry on with any straight-shooting, self-respecting decency? The friendship between Big and Texas is established upon the fact of Texas being big in the sense of being biggest: The Biggest State in the Union. All the way from trucks to tomboys, everything's big in Texas because bigger is better and Texas is best being the biggest. Until January 3, 1959 . . .

Well, to the question of how Texas might possibly carry on not being the Great Union's Goliath, there was not a yipping cowboy or ki-aying cowgirl in the land could rightly say. There were some notions, of course: Why not saddle up and expand our border down Mexico's way? Or, why not bargain with some Canadian Mountie pardners—get 'em to capture Alaska and turn it into some kind of providence or whatever they do up there? Maybe we could bargain with our beef? I donno, pardner, you think Canadians eat beef? Well, if not, they've got to like burritos which we'll have lots of after conquering all of Mexico.

In any case, by all indications (cowboy blues, saddle sore sorrows, etc.), Texas suddenly looked like a state with its dignity dismounted and its tail tucked way between its legs, head hanging low with shame.

However, with the happiness of a Sunday morning hymn, a rumor in five-part harmony began to sing throughout the jealous state of second place proportions. The chorus, in various shades of accents and feelings and tune-lessnesses, pretty much went something like this:

Listen up pardner howdy hey
Alaska ain't so big as they say.
Listen up pardner and know
Alaska is all made of melting snow!

Exactly from whence such a rumor (and such a purty song) did come—a matter of much speculation and disagreement for sure—really doesn't matter particularly. The important point is the fact that all good Texans (upstanding citizens and outlaws alike) took it to heart like cow fat that Alaska was a cheat: its materials were illegitimate, it was just a big ice cube.

So, like the silver medal swimmer who discovers that his rival's mother is a dolphin, Texas didn't go sulking in the kiddy pool but was able to maintain a bit of dignity. It's not fair to have flippers in the family in any friendly competition; it's not fair to have a state made of chilled precipitation.

Considering the importance of Texas' dignity, and considering the Texas Big hatred which all good Texans harbored in their souls for any bloated state (back off, California), it's not too difficult to imagine the ease with which Texans were able to overlook evidence which was incongruous with their state anthem (that was, the new icy rumor). Pardner, Alaska is made of snow. You say you seen a picture of trees up there? Pardner, do trees grow in soil made of snow? Course not.

Anyhow, there also was another rumor which went along with and maybe even preceded this first one. It went something like this: Due to the big (Texas-style) distance from the equator, the sun looks upon the pale countenance of Alaska in such a reticent school-boy manner during the winter months that its confident million-dollar smile of the summer cannot even hope to affect a blush upon Alaska's cute, fair cheeks. In other words: The snow never melts in Alaska.

Dah-gum! *The snow never melts in Alaska*, thought pardner Rusty Blake with a shiver one brisk Austin evening, trying to comprehend the profundity of it all. *The snow never melts in Alaska. In Alaska, pardner, the snow never melts . . .* The words could have been written in the Good Book, such was their overpowering force. Suddenly, pardner Blake jumped to his feet, grabbed his hat, saddled his horse, and rode off into the sunset, hollering at the top of his bull-riding reverberaters, "The snow never melts in Alaska!"

Rusty Blake: a notorious Texas cowboy and honest outlaw with some screwy schemes, dreams, steak recipes, and political connections. Perhaps you have heard of him? A story or two has certainly been told in his honor, ma'am. Most particularly, he earned a name for himself as the President Pardner of The Society of Pardners to Make Texas Bigger. Although The Society existed before the third of January, 1959, the rowdy members never gained much public support until after that date. Lobbying for the construction of bigger buildings, mountains, lakes, steaks, and whiskey bottles, while surely important, somehow just didn't seem terribly pressing to a public already safely situated in The Land of Big. However, with the birth of Alaska, the old homestead's very integrity was threatened. The Society of Pardners to Make Texas Bigger was thereby legitimized with a truly urgent objective: to honestly and out-rightly make Texas BIGGER.

Once a week, The Society of Pardners gathered at a local saloon where the steel guitars played their heavy-hearted country blues all night long. Among many other brilliant bits of proposed outlaw legislation, it was here that the notion of the Mexico invasion was first born.

"And after Mexico, pardners, who's to stop us from saddling up for Central and South America!" proclaimed The Society's most respected and always level-headed leader, Pardner Blake himself.

One stormy February evening, which began with Rusty Blake appearing to ride off into the sunset while, in fact, he was really heading for the Saddle Up Pardner Saloon, Pardner Blake gave his most (if not *the* most) brilliant speech in political\outlaw history.

"Pardners!" began Old Blake with the sort of authority that made even his own mustache feel unworthy. "They say that Alaska is all just made of snow!" A cold hush, like how hamburger feels being wrapped up and stuck in the ice chest, fell over The Society. The steel guitars turned frigid in their twanging. The good whiskey, though, still burned. Bottoms up!

"They also say," Blake continued, "that the snow never melts in Alaska." Another chilling thought. Brr! Drink up! "Well, pardners, I been thinkin'. And I reckon we been overlookin' somethin'. The way I figure, all we gots to do is find some way to get that derned snow to melt! I say that if the sun ain't big enough for the job, then some Texas Pardners had better saddle up!"

Sir, you can imagine the wild Texas excitement of The Society at this great pronouncement from their worthy president. Chairs flying. Glasses crashing. Voices hollering. Hear hear! Hey hey! Yip yip! Yippee-o! Saddle me up, pardner!

That very evening, The Society of Pardners to Make Texas Bigger became, with unanimous approval, The Society of Pardners to Melt Alaska. Read it in the newspapers! Listen on the radios! The five o'clock news! Hear ye, hear ye! Alaska, you big Texas toothache snow face, you better watch out: they're comin' for ya!

Pardner Joe, Pardner Riley of the rodeo, Pardner Billy, Pardner Jimmy, Pardner Paul Payton III, Pardner Herman and his brother Pardner Henry, Pardner Lou, Pardner Tim, Pardner Rick with his cowboy whip, Pardner Tom, Pardner Cody, Pardner Carter . . . in fact, every last pardner of The Society of Pardners to Melt Alaska so indeed did saddle up the very next morning on the great snow-melting mission.

"Alaska's a big place," said a newspaper interviewer to Rusty Blake as he started off out of town with his noble posse (going north).

"I reckon," said Rusty.

"How do you suppose you'll melt so much snow?"

"Ain't sure."

"Gonna build a fire, maybe?"

"I reckon," said Rusty.

Meanwhile, some of the pardners already had their worries. Pardner Tom shivered nervously at every gentle hint of breeze a-blowing from the north because the snow never melts in Alaska. Pardner Herman felt his toes growing numb because the snow never melts in Alaska. Pardner Jimmy feared for his wife and kids because the snow never melts in Alaska. Pardner Joe said a quick prayer for his trusty steed because the snow never melts in Alaska.

Pardner Tim chewed his finger nails—

Pardner John chewed tobacco—

Pardner Riley sneezed—

Pardner Bob drank—

Pardner Jack missed his cow Bessie—

. . . because in Alaska, pardner, the snow never melts.

And it was a moonshine song long ways north. Giddy up!

Well, pardner, I ain't sure precisely how to say this. You know, I'd rather not break any poor feller's heart with such bad news. But, well, to tell the truth, giddy up as they all so well did, in the end, the journey was just too much for The Society of Pardners to Melt Alaska. It turns out that taking a horsy through the States—the Rockies and all—in the sore-throat dead of winter ain't so easy as wrestling cattle in the friendly July sun while apple pie warms in the oven. In fact, there ain't no piece of pie about it.

So, of all the brave pardners, how many of 'em died and how many of 'em turned back and how many of 'em met beautiful maidens along the way and settled down to live happily ever after with two kids, a dog named Woof, and a white picket fence? Exactly how that all worked out would be hard to say. All that's known for certain is that no horsy of The Society of Pardners to Melt Alaska ever did set hoof upon the Great Alaska Highway except for the hoof of the horsy of Rusty Blake.

"Giddy up, now," Rusty said to his half-dead horse. "It's just you and me, pardner." Weary and worn out, but for the good of Texas still determined, Pardner Blake pushed on ahead.

Round about the beautiful town of Chetwynd, British Columbia, Rusty Blake dismounted with a despondent kind of glint in his cowboy eyes. He was confused. The further north he'd been traveling, the warmer it'd been getting. Of course it wasn't February any longer. He'd been traveling so long, who knew what month it might be. April? May? July, even? Yet, nonetheless, if he were anywhere near approaching Alaska, he figured it should be getting colder.

So, Pardner Blake dismounted, poked his nose in a general store, and asked a question which, out of Big Texas pride, he'd determined to never ask: "Howdy, pardner," he said. "How far you reckon it is, say, from here to uh . . . Alaska?"

The store clerk scratched his bald head and said that it was quite a long ways.

"Well, tarnation," said Blake, heavy-hearted.

"Whatcha going up to Alaska for?" asked the clerk.

"Gonna build me some sort of campfire, I reckon."

"Camping, eh?" said the clerk. "That'll be nice. Awfully good camping up there during the summer."

"Is that so?" Blake asked. "What's so derned special about the summer?"

"Well, the snow is all melted by then."

Now, by this point in his great snow-melting mission, Pardner Blake had indeed experienced the likes of delirium and confusion, once even mistaking a mountie for a moo cow. But never before had he been quite so worried for the state of his sensory devices.

"Pardner," he said, "maybe I'm going crazy, but I thought I just heard you say that the snow melts in Alaska."

"That is what I said," answered the clerk, right then a little confused himself.

"What do you mean?" Blake demanded. "Don't be foolin' with me, pardner. What do you mean the snow melts in Alaska?"

"Well, you know . . . " stammered the poor clerk, unfamiliar with the nature of certain Texan rumors. "It warms up. The snow goes away."

"The snow goes away, but Alaska is still there?"

"That's right . . . And it's a beautiful countryside." The poor fellow was trying to be helpful.

"You know this for sure?" asked Blake, his knees about to give way beneath him. He removed his old Stetson like before a funeral service.

"Pretty sure. I lived up in Anchorage for fifteen years, give or take a few months, perhaps."

Rusty Blake politely thanked the store clerk for the information, pinched himself, purchased a muffin, and saddled up again. No, he wasn't turning back. Not after having come so far. He was going to Alaska, boy. He was going to see for himself.

Moseying on into the downtown parts of Tok, AK, sometime in late spring, Pardner Blake couldn't deny the reality of the solid dirt under his horsy's tired hoofs.

Knocking upon a stranger's door, he found a bed and slept for a month. Then he continued on to Anchorage where he eventually settled down. His first night in town, he stopped in at a bar and drank to himself: the biggest outlaw cowboy in the biggest city of the biggest state in the Union. And you ain't never seen such a smug cowboy in all your days, Texas old pardner.

Anyhow, so much for The Society of Pardners to Melt Alaska. Rusty Blake moved on to bigger and better schemes of genius. Alaska is nice, after all, but not perfect by any igloo land stretch of the imagination. The first real day of Alaska fall chill hadn't even come around before Pardner Blake founded The Society of Pardners to Make Alaska Less Chilly. Once a week they gathered to discuss the feasibility of attracting tropical currents and Sahara breezes rather than snow-shoeing tourists.

Meanwhile, most Texans have generally come to appreciate the genuine landmass of mighty Alaska. Rusty Blake sent postcards.

> *Howdy, pardners. These here are real Alaskan trees with their roots in dirt so rich the first ten feet of snow looks brown. And don't even think about Mexico. I've already wrestled up a gang of pardners willing to saddle up and charge into the Yukon and them other provinces too, if need be.*

Texas sent back its own postcards with pictures of tumbleweed-cactus-juice-scorching-hot-sunny-days. Alaska had never seen such things—postcards so big.

ESSAYS

JOE WILKINS

Eight Fragments from My Grandfather's Body

Coyote Bait

I touch my grandfather's hand, trace the seam of scar that runs his palm from wrist to pinky. The mark is ragged, loud and white against his sun-dark skin. Beneath, the flesh is ridged and drawn, hard to the touch. The cyanide shell, shot from a powdered coyote-getter gun, practically tore his hand in half.

I have heard the story many times: He's setting the gun near a sheep-kill along the north bank of Willow Creek, when it accidentally fires. There's blood and black poison all over his hands and his boots, blood splashing in the dust, and his daughter, my mother, just a skinny kid of thirteen, is screaming. He's calm. He says, *Swede*—short for sweetheart, what he always calls her—*just settle down and drive, drive me on in to town now, Swede.* She listens, he lives, and I know my grandfather was lucky or strong. For though I am young, maybe five or six, I have seen sheep drop with a bullet to the ear, the belly laid open, what was inside laid out, and I know there is death somewhere back of this scar.

My grandfather grins at me, suddenly wraps his hand around my finger like a vice. His gray eyes, not stone but blue-green and silver, like sage, light as he twists my arm up and around and behind my back. He says it'll take more than a bit of coyote bait to put this old boy under and holds for a second longer, then lets go. I rub my arm, careful to look down so he does not see my watery blue eyes. He's always giving me Indian burns, putting me in head locks, pinching the backs of my arms a little too hard—but I love him anyway. Love him because the barrel-chested fathers of my friends and the old men drinking coffee at the Lazy JC Mercantile and Donny Kicker who runs the sawmill down by the river all look at me strangely. I talk more than a child should and have been put up in the higher grades for math and reading at school, and my mother went to college. But this one man, uneducated and burly as any of them, my grandfather, whose crib was a shoebox on a woodstove, who sat on the jug when his daddy ran whiskey, who's broke a thousand horses and been struck by lightning twice, does not care. He grins and tosses me into the world of scars and bodies, the world of cyanide shells and sheep-kills, the world of his dark hands. There is the craggy bark of the cottonwood in front of the house, the soft brown shag on the front room floor, and my grandfather's hands, tough as worked leather.

Come on pardner, he says, clapping me hard on the back. *Let's go get some grub.*

80 Proof

They are men in their prime—rifles slung across broad backs, grinning winks at wives and children, antelope blood all over blue jeans. The men, my father and three of his college buddies, say my brother and I, at six and eight, are too young for the hunt—*You'll have to ride with your grandfather.* I am indignant, sure that my successful summer of prairie dog hunting with the old .22 caliber, bolt-action Winchester passed down from my grandfather qualifies me to ride with them. And I am stunned that my grandfather, an expert tracker and the best rifle shot in the county behind Buster Knapp, stands for what amounts to a day of babysitting. But we three ride together in Old Blue, my grandfather's flatbed Ford, following the men down draws and coulees, over the snapping bunchgrass and sage of the prairie, despite my protests.

My grandfather drives slowly across the hills of eastern Montana, across these nine sections of the Big Dry he calls his own. And he tells us stories. Like the one about skinning squirrels for stew in the dirty '30s, or the coyote he once shot at nearly four hundred yards running. He drives on and tells us that wild game is fine meat cooked on the stove with plenty of pepper, and even better over a pine fire. With a flick of his wrist he slips his glasses off his face so he can clearly see the prairie. Since he was very young he has been farsighted and now, somewhere in the distance, he spots a buck antelope with a freak horn that swings back at the tip instead of forward. He hands us the binoculars so we, his grandsons with the nearsightedness of their bookish mother, can take a look. Sometime after lunch, as the sun swings to the west, he says that he doesn't have it in him anymore, that he's done hunting, that he believes he'll leave off the killing.

I half-listen, angry and uncaring, hoping that someone will soon rectify the injustice done to me today. But no one seems to notice, and we follow the men as they fill their tags in turn, then, when night falls, we follow them to the camphouse. It is cold and inky dark outside, clouds obscuring the stars. But the cabin is fire-warm and lit with flickering oil lamps. My brother and

I get a bottle of root beer apiece and are told to sit at the table, to pet the barn cat, to watch out for the cracking heat of the wood stove. But the men do not let my grandfather sit with us. They crowd around him, call him *Mr. Maxwell*, nearly tripping over themselves telling him about the particulars of each of their kill shots. They roll him a cigarette. They offer him a beer. He waves off both, saying, *I quit for the boys' grandmother, and I don't drink nothing if it ain't 80 proof.*

They all laugh, light up, and ask for stories.

My grandfather tilts his battered gray cowboy hat back on his bald head and tells them about skinning those same squirrels for stew in the '30s, and even before he finishes explaining the particulars of the old .22 caliber, bolt-action Winchester he hunted with, my brother and I are asleep. Later, I half wake as someone carries me out to the truck. The road home is dirt and gravel and rocks me in and out of dreams. I hear my grandfather. I try hard to pull myself from sleep. I want to listen now. Again I see the light in their eyes, the eyes of grown men, at his stories. As if they were asking a blessing. But sleep pulls me back, and a soft light grows on the far prairie, and there are great herds of antelope, and I am walking through them, touching their hard and ragged horns.

A Cheating So-And-So

My father dies when I am nine years old. My mother is now a widow with three hundred acres of farm land along the Musselshell River and three young children. My grandfather is an old man, seventy-three, but he does what he can for us. Tonight, he is teaching my brother and me to play poker. It is April, lambing season, late in the evening, and we're sitting at the kitchen table, killing time as we wait to make the midnight pass through the sheep shed, checking for ewes in labor. My grandfather deals a game of stud—and his face is suddenly stone. My brother, only seven, squeals with delight at a pair of threes, so my grandfather bets him up and clears him out with two jacks.

My mother has long since gone to bed, and my grandfather leans back, laces his fingers behind his head, and tells us that he nearly shot a man once. It was just after he'd quit school and started cowboying for Frank Schuster out of Broadview, out on the Comanche Flats. One night a bunch of cowboys and hired men were at the poker table, and this fellow was winning hand after hand. My grandfather says, *I saw that cowboy slip an ace from under his arm, and I stood up, drew my gun on him, and called him a cheating so-and-so.* He pauses and rubs the gray stubble along his jaw. *My Uncle Okie,* he continues, *he stood up beside me and hit me in the face. Knocked me clean out. I woke later that night, Okie telling me not ever to do a damn fool thing like that again.*

My grandfather is silent for a long while, his hands still clasped behind his balding head. Then he stands, tells us it's time, and we follow him out into the night. He flicks on the soft lights of the sheep shed, and we walk through the herd. We find a ewe down in the dry straw near the back. She is straining hard. We wait and watch, but the lamb's not coming. My grandfather tells us to keep an eye on her as he walks back across the shed to the wash basin and rolls up his sleeves. I glance over at him and am shocked by the sudden white splash of skin above his wrists. He washes slowly, deliberately, all the way up to his elbows. He doesn't dry his hands, just walks towards us, the drip and steam of water running from his fingers, rising from his arms.

We all kneel down beside the ewe. My grandfather tells us to hold her. *Talk to her,* he says. So we do. We tell her it will be all right. We look at him as he reaches in and say it again, *It'll be all right.* His right hand, then wrist and forearm, disappear. His movements are careful, delicate. The ewe lays her head on the straw, closes her eyes to the pain. And my grandfather pulls and pulls—and like that the lamb slips into his hands, hands that nearly took a man's life, and there's blood and afterbirth steaming on the straw, on his arms, everywhere. He runs a finger through the lamb's mouth and sets it near its mother's warmth.

We rise, stiff and suddenly very tired. My grandfather washes up. He turns off the shed lights and walks out into a darkness that is broken only by the faint light of stars. Again, we follow him.

A Hard Run Across the Flats

We walk down the fence line, hot wind in our lungs and the white hot sun in the sky. We have left the pickup at the corner of the pasture, carried our hammers and pliers and staples in steel buckets, and walked the fence today. The hardpan gumbo cracks beneath our steps, and I ask him for the story about his horse, Nine Spot. He looks down the long miles of fence, over swells of bunchgrass and a dry creek, and we sit, our backs against an old railroad tie corner post. He pulls from his pocket cheese sandwiches and plums wrapped in thick brown paper and still cold. He tells me Nine Spot was an ornery little mare, blue-black and fast. He tells me he was working for his uncle, riding for strays out on the Comanche Flats. And now it's 1931 and he is young, just sixteen, but he's already quit school to cowboy for a living, and he lets Nine Spot go at a gallop not for any reason other than they both loved a hard run across the flats.

And I know this story already, know something spooked Nine Spot— sometimes it's a snake, other times a wrong step near a gopher hole—but my young grandfather always falls from the saddle, his foot twisted in the stirrup. Nine Spot is scared, still running. My grandfather's lost his hat, feels his shirt tear and slip over his shoulders. His leg stretches and snaps. Nine Spot turns and bucks him free and keeps running, and my young grandfather lies then in the desolate heart of the flats, broken and utterly alone, the dust settling down around him and on him. This is the part I want to hear, so I lean into his breath as he grabs hold of a sagebrush, pulls himself up to it, grabs another, pulls, then another, and over a mile later he collapses in the gravel of Pretty Prairie Road, where Ollie Johnson, the Maytag repairman out of Billings, finds him hours later. My grandfather wakes as Ollie hauls him into his Model-T. His jeans are torn, and he can see the bright bone spurred through the meat of his thigh. My grandfather reaches down to touch the torn end of his own femur—and ends his story.

My heart's racing. I watch him get up, an old man again, and walk down the fence line, raising small clouds of dust. I see the hitch in his step, one leg an inch or two shorter than the other ever since the doctor set the bone wrong. And now he leans on a wood post, turns to me, and adds something that I have never heard before—*It hurt like hell, pulling myself across the ground like that. It would've been awful easy just to lay myself down and look at the sun.*

This comes like a cold north wind that snaps the grass and freezes the horse trough hard.

My world does not have to be this way. It was won for me years ago out on the prairie. I stare at my child's hands. These hands that are mine—but his as well. If he dies out there on the Comanche Flats all those years ago, I die too. His bent body—sun-dark, seventy-odd years of wind and dust—is somehow my body.

Before the Sun

Your dad and I had a deal. He was going to take charge of the whole place in a few years. And he knew how to do things right. All these ranchers around here selling off their land. Not your dad. He would've kept it up and made it pay. Two years now since my father passed, and my grandfather still grieves. We are driving again out into the distances of the Big Dry. He sits forward in the bench seat and scans the prairie as we rumble over miles of dirt road. I lean into the passenger side door and watch ropes of dust rock across the truck floor. Now and then I steal glances at him: cowboy hat cocked back on his head, dark and whiskered face, meaty hands flexed, swinging the black wheel. As we near the camphouse, he shifts Old Blue into low and lunges through Willow Creek in a splash of mud and stagnant water. A hard spring storm tore the bridge out years ago. Now there is this sudden chasm, the banks washed bare and clean.

My grandfather is seventy-five, and I am eleven, and we are going out to fix the endless miles of fence that ribbon his six-thousand-acre cattle ranch. He has told me many times that this was the ranch he saved for as he cowboyed under another man's brand through the sun and dust of the Comanche Flats, the ranch he dreamed of as he hauled one-hundred-pound sacks of wheat, one in each hand, through the long nights of harvest at the string of elevators he worked in Wheat Basin, Billings, and Dutton. Today, he eyes me and spits, says his own father was a bootlegger and gambler, hard on his wife and harder on his kids, who never owned an acre he didn't neglect, letting the cattle overgraze and the fences fall, and always losing it in a poker game. He tells me he swore he'd do things differently, do right by his family, do right by his land when he was a man, and that by 1954 he had saved enough money to buy these nine sections of pasture and build a camp house near the banks of Willow Creek. He registered his own brand as the Lazy Shamrock, to please his Irish wife, and bought the three hundred acres of cropland along the Musselshell River a few years later. He tells me how he worked hard and kept the books and made it all pay time and again, raising up his family and eventually sending all four of his kids off to college, and how, when the work got to be too much, he made a deal for the hay farm with his son-in-law and brought his daughter, and his grandsons, back to the prairie.

Even at eleven years old I know these things, these stories of the ranch, my grandfather's ranch. I have heard them told many times and somewhere deep in me I also have a sense, a bit of blood-knowledge, that this place, where Willow Creek arcs and tumbles through the soap-clean smell of sage, is my grandfather, and he is this place, and the only man, besides himself, that he trusted to run it right was my father. The sun blisters in the sky, and we stretch the wires tight against the posts and clamp them down hard. We eat lunch and walk miles and miles, and by late afternoon we're covered in dust. My grandfather slaps at his jeans and breathes deep. As the sun slips behind the far blue mountains, we drive the gravel road home.

It is only a few months later that my mother sits us down and tells us that he has sold the ranch. Without telling anyone, not his sons or his daughter, my grandfather has up and sold our land, keeping only enough to run a few cattle on. No one knows what to say. My uncles call and call, trying to figure it. My mother cries and cries, then puts our alfalfa fields up for lease as well. Everyone, it seems, is heartbroken—but I am happy. I know that my grandfather is too old, my father is dead, and now I am free. It's as simple as that. So I read and read and fall in love with worlds I have never even seen. I make plans to travel, talk earnestly about the merits of various universities. My grandfather watches as different men sign the lease papers and take their shot at making it on our hay farm. He notes if they keep up the fences, if they make it to the fields before the sun. And finally, when they move on—they always move on—he shakes his head.

Your dad would've had those ditches scraped in April and the first cutting up by May, he says, and then drives out, with a load of brand new steel posts, green and gleaming in the dawn light, to fix fence on what land he has left.

You Ready?

I am sixteen and driving fast down Highway 12. My younger brother and Justin, a skinny kid who stays with us when his uncle beats on him, are in the backseat taking pulls of cheap vodka straight from the bottle. Amy Wilson, dark-eyed and slender and beautiful as moonlight, is sitting next to me. Justin hands me a beer. I pop the top and take a long swig. Amy smiles and the stars go wild in the sky. I drop the pedal to the floor. We hurtle through engine grind and frog song, beer foam and brash laughter, and finally skid to a gravelly stop in front of our house. My mother's gone for the weekend. My grandparents live just a quarter mile down the road, but my brother and I tell everyone not to worry. *Just keep it quiet.* Then, for what seems like hours, there is only the smooth line of Amy's shoulders, her hair falling across her face. But too soon she's gone, always careful to beat her father—still holding his stool to the sawdust floor of the Sportsman Bar—back home, and B. J. Murnion shows up with some girls from Roundup, three cases of beer, and a shotgun. Stars explode across the sky.

And then it's early in the morning, not quite 6 a.m., the sun just a rim of light in the east.

Someone's knocking on something. Knocking hard, rattling glass. I swing open the front door, and my grandfather hands me a bucket of staples and a pair of fencing pliers. *You ready?* he asks. *There's miles of fence to be walked up north.*

We drive north. All morning he idles behind me in the truck as I hammer staples and hold my aching head. By noon, I'm delirious. He lets me rest for a bit, then walks with me as we string wire and rip up rotten wood posts, the hot sun hanging heavy in the sky. My grandfather, even at eighty, walks the prairie fast and sure. I straggle behind.

Blue, to Further Blue

My grandfather and I are driving through the Bull Mountains up to the Klein Creek Mine for a load of coal, and this time I am telling him stories. He listens, proud of all the things I've done off at college. I keep talking, and he indulges me, lets me ramble about theology class and our project in computer science; but, at twenty, absolutely sure that I know somewhere around ninety percent of everything there is to know and that I'll pick up the other ten percent soon, I don't quite understand that he is humoring me. He nods and chews a toothpick, his right arm hooked out the open window of the pickup, wind on the flesh of his eighty-four-year-old face.

At the mine, we buy two tons of furnace coal from a man whose skin is smeared with soot. On the drive home my grandfather buys me a burger at the A&W in Roundup. In my zeal for social, environmental, and just about every other kind of justice out there, I've quit eating fast food. But I'm hungry and don't want to hurt his feelings, so I order a bacon cheeseburger, large fries, and a root beer float.

We pull up to the stone coal cellar in his yard. He backs the truck in, and we get out and grab big scoop shovels. I peel off my shirt and, with a gravelly crunch, sink the shovel into the greasy black hunks of coal. We shovel and shovel, and soon he tires. Then my grandmother is there, wagging her finger, telling him to take it easy. She lectures him about what his doctor said and, finally, orders him down from the pickup. My grandfather is ashamed, but he listens to his wife of sixty years. I watch him walk to the house, the familiar hitch in his step, a new bend to his once board-straight shoulders.

I don't think much of it. My world of shining ideas and college girls, the world I scrambled into off the labor of his back, is so dazzling that I fail to see the dim edges of the horizon near the sagebrush hills where the light goes from blue, to further blue, to black. I have forgotten about Indian burns and broken bones and Uncle Okie. I have no idea what has happened to that old deck of poker cards. I haven't walked even a mile of fence since I left home.

I sling another shovel full of coal to the cellar and wipe the sweat from my forehead.

Dust, Jesus, and the Wind

The musk of wet oak and wine fills the shed as I pull the bung from a barrel of Waluke Slope Sangiovese, plunge the thief into the wine, and pull out half a liter. I do acid tests and yeast starters for a small winery along the Spokane River in the mornings, then, in the afternoon, sit around with the wine maker, talking, tasting, new wine wild on my tongue. I have grown my hair long. I ride my bike back into the city after work, follow the river past the falls, my head fuzzy in the haze of summer afternoon. My room-mate and I sit on the sagging porch of our college house and chain-smoke cigarettes. He's saying something about Dostoevsky, and I tell him all my grandfather's stories.

I've fallen in love with a dark-haired girl. She's gorgeous and listens to Willie Nelson. On campus the dogwoods are furious with blossoms. At twenty-three, I think the world is still new wine, and I am drinking, drinking. Then my mother calls. The cancer's back. It's in my grandfather's throat and wrapped black around his lungs. I ask her what hospital he's in, and she says they're keeping him at home on the old leather sofa in the front room. *We can care for him best,* she says, *here at home. It's only a matter of time.*

But God, what time. Days later my mother calls again, crying down the distance. He's delirious, cursing dust, Jesus, and the wind. Hung flesh. Shit on towels. The stink of chaffing skin. White thighs and penis. His once strong body, now a ruin.

And the pain. His screams are infantile, then animal, his bones given wholly to the deep rack and howl. But my mother says his hands still flutter to the sky. Sun-dark and violent with his last strength, my grandfather's hands move in the rapture of work. Now he's stretching fence, swinging out his lariat, pulling, gently pulling, the new lamb from the emptiness of air. Then he grabs my mother's wrist, looks her in the eyes with wounded recognition, says *Swede, it hurts. Swede, I'm dying here, can't you help me?*

The taste of wine like ashes on my tongue. I scatter books across the floor, read my poets for their beautiful lies, try to dream his stories. Then I'm home, and the smell of sage is strong in the spring air. My brother and I wake at dawn and drive out onto the prairie. We stop in a swirl of dust and walk into the wind and sun, look far out into the distances. My mother once told me that Jim Maxwell's heaven was just a little north and west of Willow Creek, and we know this is holy ground. We can feel it with each step, his footfalls now our footfalls. We pluck fence wire and wrap our fingers around pine posts—our hands, which were his for so long, now wholly our own. We say very little. We both know he has given everything over to us—dark hands and breath and bones. We leave this swath of prairie for a final time and drive home.

Near dusk, along with four of our cousins—his grandsons, now nearly all grown into men—we carry my grandfather over bunchgrass and pear cactus to the crest of the hill. Dust rises from our steps. Lightly, we set his broken body down.

ROBERT REBEIN

Feedlot Cowboy

I set the alarm on my cell phone for 3:45 a.m., but anticipation had me up and throwing hay to the horses half an hour before that. Bill Hommertzheim, manager of the southwest Kansas feedlot where I planned to spend the day as a pen rider, had told me to report for work at 6:30 sharp, and since the ranch where I was staying was every bit of one hundred miles away, I knew I'd have to get an early start if I was going to make it on time. While the horses ate, I checked over the saddles and other tack I had loaded onto the flatbed of the ranch truck the evening before. I was nervous in that way one gets when hurrying to make a flight at a far-off airport. Had I left myself enough time? What if I forgot something or had a flat tire? Beneath this veneer of nervousness, however, I felt a deeper layer of raw excitement for what I was about to do, together with a kind of smug satisfaction that it was I and no one else who had come up with the idea.

Half an hour later, I had entered a thick fog on the correction line between Dodge City and Cimarron. The black top was narrow and unmarked. Within ten seconds of entering the full thickness of the fog, I could see maybe a hundred feet in front of me. I had to downshift from fifth to third just to keep the truck out of the ditch. Leaning over the truck's steering wheel, I rubbed at the inside of the filthy windshield with a shop rag, hoping to work some kind of miracle. At the rate I was going, I would reach the feedlot at 7:00 a.m. or later, thus proving to Bill and whatever help he had assembled there that I wasn't even capable of showing up to work on time, let alone riding pens and scouting cattle for disease or other trouble.

The idea had come to me a few days before, when my family and I were headed west from Kansas City on one of our frequent visits to the cattle ranch my parents owned northeast of Dodge City. Somewhere near Emporia, we happened to drive past a big commercial feedlot—one of those massive, open-air animal feeding operations ("AFO" is the industry acronym) where tens of thousands of head of cattle are fed a steady diet of corn and antibiotics in the months before they are shipped to slaughter.

"God, what's that smell?" my teenage daughter said, fanning the air in front of her nose with the paperback she was reading. My son, all of ten, looked out his window and asked, in that way he still had that assumed I possessed the answers to everything, who those men were and what they were doing out there.

"What men?" I asked.

"Those," he said, pointing. "Are they cowboys?"

I craned my head to see what he was talking about. Here and there amid the acres of penned cattle, a few solitary figures with wide-brimmed straw hats could be seen moving about on horseback.

"Pen riders," I said. "Feedlot cowboys."

"Are they real cowboys?" Jake asked.

"I don't know," I said. "I guess that depends on what you think a real cowboy is."

Here the boy sighed, impatient with the wishy-washiness of the answer. "Come on, Dad. Just tell me. Are they real or not?"

"All right, they're real," I said. "No question about it. Satisfied?"

"Yes," he said, his attention already shifting from the feedlot to the gunfire and explosions taking place on his Gameboy.

I thought that would be the end of it, but as we continued on our way, I lingered over the question. What was a real cowboy—especially in this day and age? What qualified a person to be called by the name? Was it a question of clothes, attitude, allegiance to some idea or other?

Surely a mastery of horses came into the equation somewhere. Cattle, too, obviously. After all, historically speaking, wasn't the herding and safe delivery of cattle the cowboy's whole reason for existing? Gradually, a definition of sorts began to form itself at the front of my brain.

A cowboy is someone who tends cattle from horseback every day of his working life. The precision and tidiness of the definition pleased me to no end. Of course, by this standard, almost none of the people I knew, including several who spent tens of thousands of dollars a year on horses and tack, were real cowboys. I myself didn't come close to qualifying. Did I even want to? It was an interesting question.

"What are you thinking about now?" my wife asked after a couple of miles. "I don't like the look you're starting to get on your face."

"What look?" I asked.

"You know the one," she said. "Devious grin, eyebrows raised, ideas sprouting willy-nilly."

"I don't know what you're talking about," I said.

That evening, after we made it to the ranch, I called Bill Hommertzheim, a relative by marriage of my older brother David, and asked him what he thought about my riding pens for a day at the feedlot he managed near Scott City.

"I don't give a shit," Bill said in that blunt way he had, as if there were no man living who was smarter and tougher than he was, and the rest of the world had better get used to it. "I'll tell you what, though," he continued. "You've got to pull your weight and put in a full day's work. No taking little writing breaks, or cutting out of here early, or shit like that. You got to toe the line, just like all the rest of us. You don't, and we'll sure as hell run you off the place."

I could feel myself bristling inwardly at the challenge contained in these words, which I knew to be more than half bluster.

"Oh, I'll pull my weight," I said. "Don't worry about that."

"Good!" Bill said. "We'll see you at six-thirty sharp."

At 5:40, with seventy-five miles still left to go, my prayers were answered, and the fog began to lift. A few miles after that, I turned north on a good, two-lane road, and the fog dropped away completely. I shifted up from third to fifth, putting the hammer down on the pickup's 24-valve Cummins engine.

Now we're getting somewhere, I thought.

I felt like William Hazlitt in his essay "The Fight," or maybe Ivan Turgenev in "The Execution of Tropmann." I would go and I would witness, and what I witnessed would become . . . well, we would see about that, wouldn't we?

* * *

Among ranchers of my father's generation, Bill Hommertzheim will forever be "Homer" or "Homey," a hard-working kid from the plains who played some football for St. Mary of the Plains College in Dodge City before learning the feedlot trade and perfecting it with that mad science for organization and attention to detail all Germans from farm backgrounds carry inside themselves like a disease. Never mind that Bill is closer to sixty than fifty, and sorely in need of double knee replacement surgery, and talks a little more than is seemly for a true dyed-in-the-wool German. He is still Homer for all that, a hero of both the gridiron and the feedlot, a rare accomplishment indeed.

Depending on which side of the legend you believe, the Great American Cowboy who came north with herds of Texas longhorns in the 1870s and

1880s was either a violent, hard-drinking, pistol-toting miscreant, or else a congenial, soft-spoken "cavalier of the plains" who understood horses and cattle and was unfailingly kind to women and small children. It goes without saying that both halves of the legend are bogus. Historical cowboys were defined not by personality traits or social vs. anti-social tendencies, but rather by the dirty, demanding work they performed. Common laborers, they were typically drawn from the ranks of the destitute and poor, and a fair number of them (as many as one in three, according to some estimates) were Mexican or African American. Many more were Civil War vets already well-acquainted with hardship and deprivation. As the cowboy Teddy "Blue" Abbott noted in his memoir of the trail, *We Pointed Them North* (1939), the average trail hand was "raised under just the same conditions as there was on the trail—corn meal and bacon for grub, dirt floors in the houses, no luxuries." They were men who liked to brag that they could "go any place a cow could" and "stand anything a horse could," which is to say they took a strange pride in all of the suffering they endured.

A lot of this had changed by the time Bill was growing up on a farm in central Kansas in the 1950s and 60s. The open range had been replaced by fenced pastures, the old longhorn steer with its trail-toughened meat by Angus and Herford cattle with their marbled, succulent flesh, the tiny but hardy Spanish cow-pony by bigger quarter horses bred for the show and competition ring. As for Homer, he dreamed of being a football star and maybe a high school coach, not a cowboy. However, to pay his tuition bill at St. Mary of the Plains, he did cowboy some, hiring out on a part-time basis at feedlots then springing up in a fifty-mile radius of Dodge, an experience he describes as educational in a how-not-to-do-things sort of way.

"It was awful in a lot of ways," Bill says, shaking his head. "The whole feedlot business was just starting out, and nobody knew a goddamn thing about how to keep that many animals in one place and keep them alive. Nobody knew how to ride a pen, or what to look for, or even whether or not a horse should even play a part in the work. There was no system to it at all, just cattle, chaos, and wild swings of fortune depending on all kinds of things that were out of our control. I was working at one of the bigger outfits when the Blizzard of 1978 hit. You have no idea of the destruction that caused. You needed a loader and a dump truck just to haul away the corpses. We had no idea how to doctor them, either. One cow got sick, they all got sick. I'm telling you, it was just death, death, death."

That's where Bill's special talent came into play—a talent that exceeded even his prowess at football. "One summer when I was a kid," he says, recounting a favorite story, "my aunt gave me a bunch of chickens to raise as fryers. A neighbor took one look at the box of chicks and said, 'Don't waste your time. They're all gonna get sick and die.' I said to him, 'You wanna bet? I can keep these sumbitches alive. Just you wait and see.'" Here Bill grins, remembering. "I didn't know a goddamn thing about chickens, but I was determined. I kept my eye on those birds twenty-four-seven, wracking my brains night and day thinking about what might happen to them and how I could prevent it. Long story short, when the end of the summer came and my aunt showed up to get her fryers, I hadn't lost a single bird. Not one, you understand? Well, my aunt looked at them birds, all fat and healthy, and said, 'Goddamn, Billy! How'd you do it?' 'It wasn't hard,' I said. 'You just have to pay attention.' Very few people pay attention to anything these days."

It was this talent that Bill carried into his part-time job at the feedlot. But when the time came for him to do his student teaching, he faced a dilemma of sorts. "They don't pay you for that," he says. "I had bills to pay, and I needed the teaching experience to get certified, but how was I going to get the experience if I starved to death in the meantime?" He throws his hand out before him like a punch, dismissing the memory. "I kept on at the feedlot, even after I graduated with my degree in Education."

A year or two into his feedlot career, Bill could feel a door closing behind him. He'd have made a good teacher and a better coach, but other work had claimed him, as it claims so many of us. The feedlot had entered his bloodstream. It was who he was now. Like the other pen riders, he wore a cowboy hat and boots and maintained a string of ponies to use at work. In time, he even developed his own system for how to ride a pen, what to look for and what to ignore, when to pull a cow from the herd and send it to the hospital, when to let it go another day or two. There was deep satisfaction in this work, yes, but did any of it make him a cowboy?

"You got to understand," Bill says when asked this question. "My idea of a cowboy was John Wayne. I thought well enough of myself. But John Wayne? The Duke? That's setting the bar pretty high . . . "

Hearing Bill say this, one gets the impression that in his case maybe the bar wasn't set all that high, Duke or no Duke. After all, there is image, and then there is reality, and the world of the feedlot is all about reality, day in and day out, twenty-four-seven.

* * *

By the time I rolled through Scott City, eight miles east of the feedlot, the pickup's digital clock read 6:32. It was still gray-dark outside, and from what I could see, the land in all directions was flat as a tabletop. There were no trees to speak of, and hardly any farm houses or other buildings—just wheat and corn stubble and the occasional pasture dotted with cattle, the roads running between these giant fields as straight and true as if someone had drawn them with a straight edge. I caught the smell of the feedlot before I saw anything. First a big one loomed on the right side of the road, and then Bill's, somewhat smaller, came up on my left. It was a big, flat, industrial space, nothing but pen after pen of milling, bawling cattle, with a noisy feed mill towering over one end, and greenish-black waste water ponds at the other. Light poles illuminated the scale house and the wide gravel lot at the center of the place, throwing an eerie fluorescent glow on everything that reminded me of one of those lunar mining scenes you sometimes see in science fiction movies.

Bill met me in the carpeted hallway of the feedlot's main office, a bunker-like building with a bathroom, a couple of desks with computer equipment, and a massive scale for weighing trucks.

"How the hell are you? Are you ready to go to work?" he asked, his eyes inspecting me over the tops of wire-rim glasses. He looked older than the last time I had seen him, but still hale and forceful for all that, every bit the retired footballer in cowboy boots and a xxxx Stetson.

"I'm good," I said. "How are your knees? Dave tells me you're looking at a double replacement."

"When I can get time, I am," Bill said, glancing at his watch dramatically, as if to comment on my tardiness. "Got an interesting day lined up for you. Think you're ready?"

"You bet," I said.

"Come on, then," he said. "I'll take you down to the barn and introduce you to Apache and the boys."

The barn was a squat metal building set on hardpan in the dead center of the feedlot. I parked the ranch truck on a wide gravel lot next to the building and unloaded the horses: Cuba, a ten-year-old Palomino gelding that according to Bill had been "ruined by too much roping," and Doc, a seven-year-old sorrel gelding my brother Joe had recently acquired from a man who said the horse had spent several years working in a feedlot. I saddled them quickly and led them to a pipe rail behind the barn, where four other horses stood tied, then joined Bill and the rest of the crew inside.

Snaking from one end of the barn to the other was a taper-sided crowd alley leading to a hydraulic squeeze chute. Overhead doors opened on three sides of the building, allowing a manure-tinged breeze to whisper through. Dozens of small birds nested in the rafters above the concrete floor, providing a discordant soundtrack to the place. In a corner of the building closest to where the horses were tied, a metal door gave to a small break/supply room with lockers and a big, glass-fronted refrigerator full of antibiotics and other drugs.

"This is Joaquin, also known as Apache," Bill said, indicating a tall man in his mid-thirties with steady brown eyes, high cheek bones, and jet black hair cut into a Mohawk. "Apache's been with me the longest of all these guys. What is it now, Apach? Eight years?"

"Yes, eight," Joaquin answered, reaching out to shake my hand.

"These other guys are Jose, been with me six years, Sergio, and Jaime," Bill continued as I shook each man's hand in turn. Ranging in age from nineteen to thirty, the men were all dressed in cheap, durable work clothes—feed caps, jeans bought at Wal-Mart, cotton hoodies—whereas I, by contrast, had on a straw cowboy hat, a long-sleeved Roper shirt with pearl buttons, and a pair of leather rodeo chaps.

"You'll find that none of these boys says very much," Bill said, hand on my shoulder, very coach-like. "At least not in English. But just stick by Apache, and he'll tell you what to do." He handed Joaquin a to-do list full of pen numbers and head counts and feeding regimes, and turned back to me one final time. "Any questions?"

"Yeah, what time is lunch?" I said, attempting a joke.

"After all the pens are ridden," Bill said over his shoulder, already on his way out the door and back to his office in the scale house.

After Bill was gone, Jose offered me a seat and a cup of coffee, and the five of us sat around a while in the polite, awkward silence of people who have been thrown together but do not speak the same language. There was a lot of eye contact and nodding smiles. A donut was offered, which I declined. There was so much I wanted to ask these men, I didn't know where to begin.

I wanted to ask: Are you legal? Do you like your job? How much are you paid? Do you have health insurance? How did you learn to ride? Do you consider yourself a cowboy? Do you consider this place where you work a fucking environmental disaster area? Do you have kids? What are your dreams for them? Do they play too many video games and eat too much sugary cereal? What are the best and worst parts of your day? Do you like cattle, or are they just meat to you? Do you love horses?

In the end, though, I just sat there with a dumb smile glued to my face, nodding and supplying the answers myself.

"Okay," Joaquin said, having finished the Marlboro he was smoking. "Now we go get the cattle."

We grabbed bridles and pulled the cinches on our saddles. By now the sun was up. It was a misty morning, chilly for late May. Leaving the barn, we rode down a sand alley as wide as any city street. Not a blade of grass grew anywhere. The whole place was nothing but sand and mud, fourteen-gauge steel pipe, and cattle, cattle, cattle. Black cattle, brown cattle, yellow cattle, white cattle. Big and not so big, heifers and steers. Thousands upon thousands of them, all standing around in the sand and mud, waiting for breakfast, which even then was being delivered by trucks making runs from the feed mill to the concrete feed bunks lining the pens.

Sergio and Jaime rode ahead to open a series of gates which Jose and Joaquin and I chained together to form a single, L-shaped alley leading from the far end of the feedlot back to the processing barn. Cuba, a bundle of energy as always, tossed his head and danced excitedly down the middle of the alley, calling into question my ability to control him.

"Nice horse," Joaquin offered, nodding appreciatively.

"He's a good horse," I agreed. "A little crazy, though. Caballo loco?"

"Si, caballo loco," Jose laughed. "All Palominos are that way."

Five minutes after leaving the barn, we came to the first pen on Bill's work order.

Joaquin, leaning sideways from his horse, opened the gate and held it for me as I rode through.

The simple grace with which he performed this maneuver—no motion or effort wasted, the entire thing a single, fluid movement—filled me with professional envy. Did I have a right to that envy? I didn't know. All I knew was that I wanted my own horsemanship to be like that. What would it take to get there? How many repetitions over how many days and weeks? It was a little daunting to think of, although still squarely in the realm of possibility. There was no question that Cuba was capable. But was I?

Once in the pen, we began a slow, methodical gathering of the one hundred or so cattle it contained. Moving no faster than our horses carried us at a walk, we slowly pushed the cattle out of the pen and into the alley we had built to funnel them back to the processing barn. Jaime, Jose, and Sergio rode at the point of our herd of fifty yearling steers, while Joaquin and I brought up the rear.

"When did these cattle get here?" I asked Joaquin.

"Yesterday," he answered.

"How long will they stay?"

"Six months, maybe. Until they're fat."

"What's fat?"

"Twelve hundred pounds, maybe."

"How much do they weight now?"

"Seven or eight hundred."

I paused to do the math. "So they gain what, five hundred pounds in six months?"

"A little more. The goal is three and a half pounds a day."

"That's a lot of corn," I observed.

"Yes," Joaquin agreed, smiling for the first time that day. "A lot of corn."

After herding the first group of cows into pens behind the processing barn, we rode out to the next pen on Bill's list and brought these cattle in the same way. Two more times we repeated the operation, riding out to distant parts of the roughly 640-acre yard and slowly trailing the cattle in. By the second trip, I had begun to help with the opening and closing of gates. By the fourth, Cuba had dropped his head and settled into the work. The sun had burned through the early morning mist by then. The sky was a dull gray above the level horizon. Feed trucks rumbled up and down the sand alleyways, delivering the morning ration of corn and silage.

With a capacity of sixteen thousand head, the feedlot contained five or six times the number of cows in the average herd of longhorns driven up the trail to Dodge City in the 1870s and 1880s. Still, it was a fairly small yard by industry standards. A half an hour to the west was a corporate owned yard with a capacity of over 100,000 head. Another yard to the south fed 120,000 head.

Veritable cities of cattle, these mega-yards called to mind the sprawl, crowded conditions, and large-scale pollution of a Mumbai or Mexico City. But even the relatively small feedlot we were riding had some of this feel. The feed mill supplying the place was the size of a small office building, and the removal of manure from the pens was a gargantuan task involving the use of loaders and dump trucks. From this densely complex environment an equally complex smell arose: a mixture of corn silage, cow manure, and an evil-smelling gas that was especially strong the closer one got to the black lagoons holding run-off from the pens.

By 7:15, we had gathered the last of the cattle on Bill's work order. I tied Cuba to his place at the pipe rail behind the barn, loosened his cinch, and followed Joaquin into the break room, where Jose and Sergio were drinking coffee and Jaime, seated at a table in the corner, was busy pressing lot numbers onto a stack of rubber ear tags.

I shot a look to Jose, as if to ask, "Now what?"

"Process cattle," he said, sipping at the steaming coffee.

* * *

Back in trail drive days, working cattle meant gathering them from the open range and separating the calves from the rest of the herd. One by one, these calves were roped, dragged to a fire, and branded. If the calf was male, it was castrated. If it had horns that could injure another cow, these were cut off with a hack saw or a pair of heavy clippers. The principal tools in this work were the lariat or rope, the branding iron, and the castrating knife, and even novice cowboys quickly became adept in the use of all three. With the exception of the knife, today's feedlot cowboy has no use for any of this. His "range" is a world of numbered pens and concrete-floored processing barns, and his tools are a crowd alley and squeeze chute, an implant gun for the injection of growth hormones, and, above all, a jumbo hypodermic syringe for the delivery of antibiotics and other drugs.

This is the hidden, vaguely obscene world so few Americans know anything about. In theory, yes, they know it exists. An extensive archive of activist videos awaits anyone who cares to get on YouTube to take a peek. But most people prefer not to know, or at least not to think about, where their food comes from. Growing up amid farm and ranch work, I had never had that luxury, and so, in a sense, I suffered from the opposite problem. Continued exposure to ranch and farm life had hardened me to it the way an ER doctor becomes hardened to the sight of blood and amputated limbs. To really see the world of the feedlot in all its postmodern bizarreness was an effort for me. I had to continually ask myself, "What in this picture would strike my vegan colleagues at the university as especially evil and strange?" and even then I mostly failed. We are who we are, as Homer liked to say.

As we prepared to process the cattle we had gathered that morning, Joaquin arranged tagging knife and ear tags, antiseptic wash, hormone implants, and other necessities on a little cart he wheeled into place beside the squeeze chute. Every man on the crew had a job. One man drove the cattle up the crowd alley. Another caught the cattle one by one in the hydraulic squeeze chute and gave them a couple of quick injections. A third, working on the opposite side of the chute, cut excess hair from tails (so great balls of mud wouldn't form there after a few days in the pens) and reached a gloved hand between the hind legs to make sure the males had been castrated. Joaquin, working at the front of the chute, gave each cow an implant beneath the skin of its left ear.

My job was to attach a rubber ID tag to the same ear. "Hold the tag on the knife with your thumb," Joaquin instructed me in his quiet way. "Then take the ear in your left hand, slice the tag up and through the ear, release your thumb, and pull the knife back out like this, leaving the tag in. See?"

I did see. The question was whether I could do it myself without botching the job. A second later, another cow was driven into the chute. I placed a tag on the tiny nub of metal at the end of the tagging knife and waited for Joaquin to be finished with the implant. Then I stepped in, grabbed the cow's ear, and sliced up and through it as Joaquin had shown me. However, when I removed the knife, the tag came out, too, falling at my feet on the dirty concrete floor.

Looking up at where the tag should have been, I saw only an L-shaped hole with blood dripping from it.

"You have to let go with your thumb," Joaquin said, picking up the tag from the floor and skillfully slicing it into a different part of the ear.

"Okay," I said. "I think I've got it now."

Another cow was driven into the chute. This time I let go with my thumb at the right moment, and the tag, though loose and bloody, stayed in. I stepped back, Joaquin checked my work, and the cow was released into a holding pen outside the barn.

Over and over I repeated the task, sometimes performing it flawlessly, more often mucking it up in some small or big way. By the time I had tagged twelve or fifteen cattle, my right thumb began to ache from the strain of holding the tag in place on the knife. After thirty, both of my hands ached, and I could feel the concrete floor coming up through the heels of my boots. Still the cattle kept coming, one after another. I concentrated on simplifying the motions involved in the task, so I would have more time to relax the muscles in my hands between animals. I made sure to dry my fingers on a paper towel, so that grasping the next cow's ear would be a little easier. Throughout all this, I could feel the eyes of Joaquin and the other men on me. They were sizing me up, seeing if this professor could hack it in their world. The more blood-smeared my thirty-dollar cowboy shirt became, the more they smiled and winked at each other. I did not blame them in the least for this. From what I could tell, the job of processing cattle was a case of carpal tunnel waiting to happen. It was like working on an assembly line—or in a beef packing plant. I kept asking myself, *How do they do it? How do they keep coming back for this punishment, day after day after day?* But no answer was forthcoming.

"Getting tired?" Joaquin asked with a grin, after we had processed a hundred cattle.

"A little," I said. "How about you?"

He shrugged in his stoic way, and I dug my cell phone out of my shirt pocket and glanced at the screen. Sweet Jesus! 8:45 a.m.! Back home in Indianapolis, I would be propped up in bed with the newspaper and a cup of coffee, quietly contemplating the day to come.

* * *

Bill is the only white American working at his feedlot. The rest of the feedlot staff, from the pen riders to the feed truck drivers to the front office help, are Mexican. When I asked Bill why this was, he gave me a level look and said, "The day when you could get a white man to do this job is over, son. Or if you can, you better watch out for what kind of white man he is. Pretty soon, he starts showing up to work drunk or hung over. Then things start to go missing in the supply room, and you have to start keeping everything under lock and key. And don't even get me started on lawsuits and worker's comp . . . "

Here Bill pauses. "I had this one kid come out and apply. Good looking kid, strong and clean cut, would have made an excellent linebacker. Halfway through the interview, I'm thinking, 'Maybe I've been too quick to judge these sumbucks, maybe this'll be the one to change my mind.' But then the kid looks me right in the eye and says, 'Oh, there is one thing. I can't work on Sundays. It's against my religion.' I couldn't help it. I laughed in his face.

I said, 'Son, the way I see it is this. God made these animals, and they have to eat, Sunday or no Sunday. You think Noah took Sunday off, and just let all the animals on the Ark starve to death? I don't think so. The way I see it, the feedlot is our church, and feeding these cattle is our way of praising God, and if we do a good enough job, maybe we'll get to heaven like all good Christians do in the end.' And having said that, I kicked that snotty-nosed little punk out of my office and went on back to work."

Joaquin was a roofer when he started working for Bill. He knew nothing about cattle, and had never ridden a horse in his life. But unlike the saddle bums who sometimes showed up at the scale house looking for a day's or a week's work, he had no preconceived notions about how to do the job. If Bill told him to look the same direction every time he rode pens, so that the cattle flowed past him precisely the same way, day in and day out, that's exactly what Joaquin did. He had no bad habits as a horseman, because Bill had taught him everything he knew, and Bill himself had no bad habits. As for the long hours, low pay, and lack of benefits—the same was true of roofing, beefpacking, and a dozen other jobs, none of which featured the added benefit of being able to perform at least some of the work from the back of a horse.

There's a curious, full-circle quality to this. Fifty years before there was a cattle industry in Texas or Kansas, Spanish-speaking vaqueros in California had already set the tone and established the equipment, techniques, and much of the vocabulary used in the work. The cowboy's distinctive hat, boots, spurs, and saddle are all of Spanish origin, as are many cowboy words like lariat (from *la reata*), dally (*dar la vuelta*), chaps (*chaparreras*), buckaroo (*vaquero*), and so on. Even the American quarter horse, the mount of choice among American cowboys for more than a century, can be traced in part to horses brought to the New World from Spain in the fifteenth century. Like the men who rode them, these horses were small but hardy, requiring little in the way of food or water to do a notoriously tough job.

And yet, there is a strange, otherworldly quality to all of this, too. How many Americans would guess that nine out of ten people working in feedlot and beef-packing industries in places like southwest Kansas are recent arrivals from Mexico, many of them without documentation? Most everyone in Kansas knows, of course. But America is not Kansas. Not yet, anyway.

* * *

By 10:30 in the morning, we had finished implanting, vaccinating, and tagging new arrivals at the feedlot. It was time to get back in the saddle to ride pens. This was the work I had imagined myself doing when I was first visited by the notion of spending a day working as a feedlot cowboy. However, the idea that I would be given pens of my own to ride turned out to be pure fantasy on my part. Riding pens in Bill's feedlot was precision work meant to be done according to a playbook I hadn't mastered. Rather than ride pens of my own, I had to tag along with Joaquin and try to get a feel for the work that way. Even this broke one of Bill's cardinal rules—the one against cowboys "buddying up" and riding pens together, which according to Bill only led to sloppy decision making and a lack of concentration.

"Saddle bums love to ride pens together," Bill liked to say, "and that's just one of the reasons why they suck at their jobs and usually do more harm than good. Instead of eyeballing a cow and making a decision, they sit there on their horses and talk about it. Does she look bloated to you? No? Well, maybe you're right . . . Idiots!"

We started on the east side of the feed yard, taking the pens one at a time, riding quietly in, closing the gate behind us, and then inspecting each animal as it flowed past us from right to left, looking for sluggishness, slowness to get up, runny noses or eyes, and the tell-tale signs of bloat or acidosis, a condition caused by a too rapid or over-consumption of grain.

The cattle in the first few pens were recent arrivals—fast, squirrelly animals that scampered out of our way as soon as we entered their pen. You had to be slow and steady around these cattle, so as not to spook or stress them.

"See the little black one?" Joaquin asked in a quiet voice, nodding at an undersized calf that seemed to want to hide from us, attaching itself to a bigger calf as if its mother. "How slow he's moving? We'll pull him out."

The next time the cattle flowed past us, Joaquin cut the black calf out of the herd and held him against the fence while the rest of the herd flowed to the opposite end of the pen. Then as Joaquin trotted over to open a gate to the alley, Cuba and I held him there, the horse coming to life beneath me, matching every move and fake the calf threw at him, until finally the calf had been delivered through the gate and into the alley.

"Nice," Joaquin said, nodding at Cuba. "How much you want for him?"

"Sorry," I said. "He's my brother Dave's horse. Not for sale."

"Bill says he picked the horse out himself at an auction. But then he was ruined. Too much roping."

"Yes, I know all about that," I said.

The man shrugged broadly. "He look good to me, though. We'll pick up little blackie on our way back."

The cattle in the next pen looked remarkably different from the yearlings we had just left. These were "finished" cattle, nearing the end of their stay at the feedlot. Many were lying down when we rode into their pen, and they were slow to get to their feet. Several times I had to ride almost on top of a cow to get it to move, and even then it was with the slow, stiff-leggedness of the morbidly obese.

"What about that one?" I asked Joaquin, nodding at an enormous black cow that waddled out of our way with great deliberateness. "Anything wrong with him?"

"No, just fat," Joaquin said.

But fat did not begin to describe this cow. He looked as if someone had inserted an air hose beneath his hide and inflated him to his present, blimp-like proportions. There was something awful, yet awe-inspiring, too, about this enormous beast. Looking at him was like looking at a champion body builder or a blue ribbon steer. He was a freak, to be sure, but he was also the product of an entire industry's striving for a certain kind of perfection. Not just ranchers and cowboys, but men and women in lab coats with advanced degrees from the best universities in the land had produced him. Wash the mud off his hide and give him a quick shampoo, and he'd be a good bet to win the fair.

In another pen, we came upon a similarly fat cow, only this one had what looked to be a basketball sticking out of its left side. "Is that one just fat, too?" I asked.

"No, she bloated," Joaquin said, circling the cow quietly. "We put her in the alley with the little black one."

As the morning wore on, Joaquin and I worked our way through a line of pens running parallel to those being ridden by Jose, Sergio, and Jaime. The sun was fully out now, and the cowboys had put away their feed caps and donned wide-brimmed straw hats. This was the longest and most important part of the day we would spend on horseback, and there was a pleasure in the work that for me stood in direct contrast to the feet-bound work of processing.

Every half hour or so, we would stop at a concrete water trough in the pen we were working and let our horses take a long drink. I would sit up straight in my saddle and look off in the distance, often catching sight of another pen rider silhouetted against the horizon. It was the same iconic scene my son Jake and I had spied out the window on our way west from Kansas City. Now, as then, there was something oddly grand about it. Despite the degradation of our surroundings, some small part of the romance of cowboy life continued to live on here.

Halfway through our assigned pens, I decided it was time for me to contribute something to the work we were doing. If I couldn't be trusted to determine which cattle to pull, at least I could relieve Joaquin of the necessity of opening and shutting all those gates.

The top of a rectangular feedlot gate is four and a half feet off the ground, or about as high as the average horse's shoulder. Set on hinges and made of two-inch steel pipe, the gate swings in or out and is secured by an iron slip-rod set on a 45-degree angle. Hurrying ahead of Joaquin, I rode right up to the first gate we came to, held Cuba's right side in check with my spur, and reached down with my left hand to push the gate open wide enough for Joaquin and his horse to pass through. After he had done so, I side-passed Cuba again, pushing the gate in front of us, and dropped the slip-rod, closing it. Soon I was riding ahead to open and shut every gate we came to. Maybe the action wasn't as fluid or pretty as when Joaquin did it, but it was passable work, and I felt good doing it.

Then we came upon a corner gate set on the edge of a slippery embankment with a pool of quicksand-like mud at the base of it. This was a different kind of challenge, and Cuba responded to it by being even more keyed-up and impatient than usual. Still, I managed to hold him on the embankment while I pushed the gate open before me and we stepped through. However, as I spun the horse's hindquarters around, the gate slipped from my hand and swung back into the alley with a rush, narrowing missing Joaquin and his horse.

"Shit, sorry," I said. "Let me get it."

But by then Joaquin already had the gate in his hand. "Open it this way, toward you," he said, demonstrating. "It's easier that way."

"Thanks," I said, feeling the red rise up from my neck and into my ears. As crazy and unrealistic as the desire was, I really did want to do the job on the same level as Joaquin and the others. No matter how many gates I flubbed or ear tags I dropped on the floor, the desire remained. Why? What accounted for it? I couldn't say. All I knew was that it was there inside me like some ancient and unnecessary mutation.

We pulled a dozen sick cattle during the two hours we spent riding pens that day. Only one cow was a case of acidosis. The rest were pulled for symptoms ranging from lethargy to a runny nose. These we pushed as a single herd up the main alley of the feedlot to a holding pen behind the "hospital" or doctoring barn, where Bill awaited us.

"This is the third time in the hospital for that bloat," he observed, looking over the cattle we had pulled. It was clear from watching him that every fiber in Bill's body was engaged by his work. After thirty-five years working in various feedlots, you would think the man would have grown sick of it by now. But we all tend to gravitate toward work we're good at, and Bill's special talent was keeping animals alive—right up to the moment they were shipped to the slaughterhouse to die.

* * *

We ate lunch in a hamburger joint/bowling alley in the middle of Scott City. "What do you think of my crew?" Bill asked, after our order was in.

"They're good," I said.

"Goddamn right they are," he said with a smile and a nod. "I put that team together myself, trained every last one of them. They're cross-trained. Every cowboy on the crew can drive a feed truck, and the feed truck drivers, in a pinch, can ride pens. Joaquin is the captain of the team. They're all accountable to him, and he's accountable to me. They're related, too. Sergio is Jose's little brother. Did you happen to notice that?"

"No, I didn't," I said.

Bill nodded again. "I think the world of those boys, I really do. I'd do anything for them. Of course, if they started screwing up, I'd fire them, too. You have to be that way, or they'll walk all over you."

For the next forty-five minutes, while I slammed a cheeseburger and onion rings and three Diet Cokes, Bill regaled me with stories from his career as a "fixer" of feedlots.

"You get some guy who doesn't know his head from his ass running one of these places, and he goes and hires a bunch of idiots, thieves, and other degenerates, and pretty soon the inmates are running the asylum and the cattle are standing in their own muck, sick and starving to death. Things get bad enough, the phone starts ringing. 'Homer, can you please come clean up this terrible mess we've made out here?' What can I say? It's what I do."

"Do you ever get a hankering to work for one of the really big outfits?" I asked. "A hundred thousand head? Bigger?"

"Hell, no. Those aren't feedlots. They're disasters waiting to happen. They don't even use horses in those yards. They fly over the pens in helicopters, look out the windows of pickups, shit like that. It's all a numbers game to them. Sorry, but I'm not built that way."

I finished my cheeseburger and sat there with a wide grin on my face.

"What?" Bill asked.

"You're coaching," I said, having saved up the insight for just this moment. "It's not football, but you still treat it like a game. Maybe that's why it's still fun for you."

"You know what?" Bill said, smiling broadly. "You're right about that. And I'll tell you something else, too. If we got to play in games, if feedlot cowboying was a competitive enterprise, we'd kick the ass of any other feedlot crew in the state, bar none. I'm telling you, boy. We'd run them right off the field."

"What about me?" I asked. "Would I make it off the bench?"

The man looked at me like I was crazy. "Well, maybe. After a while," he said with all the diplomacy he could muster.

* * *

The hospital was a cement-floored building the size of a large suburban garage. A high-sided crowd alley and squeeze chute similar to the one in the processing barn dominated the floor plan, which included a small room for storing veterinary supplies and a computer terminal for checking animal health records. One by one, each of the animals we had pulled that morning, as well those who remained in the hospital from the day before, were driven up the alley and into the squeeze chute, where Sergio, wearing surgical gloves, inserted an anal thermometer and Jose read the animal's tag number to Bill, who entered it into the computer.

Jose: "One oh eight five four."

Bill: "Five four?"

Jose: "Yes, five four."

Bill: "Temp?"

Sergio: "One oh three."

Bill: "A little hot. Let's give this little cow ten units of Draxxin and keep him here another day."

Upon hearing this, Sergio drew the dose into a syringe, attached a clean needle, and gave the cow an injection in the side of its neck, just above the shoulder. Then as Bill updated the cow's medical chart, Jose released him from the squeeze chute, and Sergio ran in the next cow in line.

Although neither Jose nor Sergio spoke much English, they had no trouble at all understanding Bill's instructions to them. Once, hearing Bill call for forty-four cc's of a particular drug, and seeing Sergio draw only twenty-two, I pointed out the discrepancy to him, whereupon Sergio showed me that the syringe held only thirty cc's. "I draw two times twenty-two," he explained. After that, I kept my mouth shut and watched.

When the bloated cow was run into the chute, Bill sighed and said, "She's a chronic. Probably she won't make it, but you never know."

Jose ran a length of flexible hose down the cow's throat and into its stomach while Bill and I pushed on the basketball-sized bloat on the cow's left side, causing the gas collected there to make a sharp hissing sound as it escaped through the hose.

"All right, I think that's it," Bill said.

Hearing this, Sergio patted the animal's head with something like affection, then opened the chute, releasing her into the outer corral, where Jaime stood ready to load her into a trailer for transport back to the pen from which she had been pulled a few hours before.

* * *

We finished doctoring sick cattle a little after 3:30 p.m., exactly twelve hours after I got out of bed that morning. By then I was tired enough I could have lain down on the concrete floor of the processing barn and fallen straight to sleep. Instead, we mounted back up (by now I was on Doc, my second horse of the day) and rode out into the feedlot to bring in a group of seventy-five heifers that had arrived earlier in the day. By the time we finished processing this last group and were driving them back to their home pen on the far side of the feedlot, it was after 6:00.

As we made our way back to the barn at the end of that long day, the cowboys chatted amiably in Spanish, and Joaquin performed a kind of jig on his horse, side-passing him down the middle of the alley. Watching this dance, it struck me that despite the long hours and grueling nature of the work, feedlot cowboying, at least the way it was practiced at Bill's feedlot, was still one of the few jobs left in America that a man got to do from horseback. You couldn't say that about a factory job or an office job, and God knows you couldn't say it about working in a beef packing plant. It was just this element that saved the job from mere drudgery, elevating it to a status just this side of myth.

Still, it wasn't like any of this was enough to make me want to come back and do it all over again the next day, and I told Bill as much as I was loading Cuba and Doc into the trailer for the hour and a half ride back to the ranch.

"I figured as much," Bill said, sucking on a toothpick he had saved from lunch. "I'll be here, though, and so will Joaquin and Jose and the rest. After all, cattle have to eat, even on Sunday."

I stopped to consider this. There was more to Bill's attitude, I saw now, than braggadocio and an out-of-control work ethic.

"You really do love it, don't you?" I asked. "The work, the smell, the endless, repetitive nature of the job. 'A cowboy's work is never done.' All that shit."

"Well, love's a strong word," Bill demurred, sucking at the toothpick. "But sure. I love it. Why the hell not?"

Only a cowboy could.

E.C. (Teddy Blue) Abbott and Helena Huntington Smith, *We Pointed Them North: Recollections of a Cowpuncher* (Norman: University of Oklahoma Press, 1939), 6-7.

MERRILL SHANE JONES

Hiding in the Cornrows

Josh Love and Eric Schneider are mounted up and on the lookout for movement in the tall yellow corn. "I see one now," Josh says, but I don't know how he can. As high as these cowboys sit up in their saddles, the corn's even higher, and there are 140 acres of it—enough to fill more than a hundred football fields.

"There's cows in them cornrows." That's what Farmer John says. Farmer John, who doesn't like reporters and isn't really named Farmer John. He's losing his hair, just like me, and he keeps it closely cropped as a way to limit contrast between hair and no hair, that's my guess anyway, and he's not fooling anyone.

Farmer John lost all his cows to the corn early this afternoon, trying to load them into a horse trailer. "I've done it a thousand times," he says. "Three run off before I even know it; then the rest run off." He takes his hand up flat like a crop duster taking flight. "Airborned my four wheeler over the pivot pond after two of them." He looks at me. "What? You a reporter?"

"No," I tell him.

I just want to write this down. What the hell's a pivot pond? But even though I tell him I'm not a reporter, he still doesn't like damn reporters. Says he had one come up just the other day and ask him his full name.

"'I don't know you,'" he says he told that nosy town man. "Said he needed it, had to have it, works for the paper. 'I don't know you.'"

When I was a kid growing up in Texas, we called town men *city boys*—I thought I was a cowboy back then. But now I just hope Farmer John doesn't have it in his head I'm some kind of city boy asking about full names and business I have no business asking about. For the past two hours, I've been walking the cornrows in my new cowboy boots, hunting cows. Up to now, Farmer John just assumed I worked with Josh and Eric—two cowboys from Loveland, Colorado, he hired to help find and round up his cows. Farmer John must have thought I was a cowboy, too; even though I don't have Eric's calloused workman's hands or Josh's long, assertive strides. But now I can feel a line of separation between these cowboys and me, thick as the crowded stalks I've had to cross from row to row, and for the rest of the day, Farmer John's going to think he's more like these cowboys than I am.

I put my notebook in my back pocket and throw my shirttail over it. Farmer John tells Eric about how he knows other farmers by name as far north as Billings, Montana. "Nowadays, people don't know a neighbor just two miles down the road."

"Too many people," Eric says. "All those Californians moving in."

I jump in with what I've heard a lot of people complain about. "They move in and then boost up the real estate. It's why it's so expensive to live in Boulder."

Eric nods, spits, says *yup* or something like it. Farmer John changes the subject.

"I had one cow walk off twenty-six miles," he says. "As the crow flies." He looks at me.

"She didn't really walk as the crow flies. She had to go through my neighbors' properties, walk around fence lines. There was obstacles." Farmer John thinks I'm stupid. He looks at Eric who has a goatee with neatly trimmed edges like where the pasture meets the corn. Eric has a pinch of dip centered in his bottom lip and he just kind of throws his chin up and lets the tobacco juice lob out in a stream. He looks down at Farmer John from up on his horse, would still be looking down if he was on foot, down at both of us.

Farmer John continues. "She ended up twenty-six miles as the crow flies on the side of the highway, and I get a call from a neighbor. I drove the twenty-six miles. Couldn't find her. She comes back the next day and walks straight for the feed yard. That was just the other day." Farmer John tells other stories and they all happened just the other day.

We haven't been able to find any cows in the corn. There's too much of it. I ask him how long the cows might be in there and he's slow to answer, sizing up this town man with a tilt of his head and a slight purse to his lips. I notice growth like specs of black dirt on his face and feel my own, think I could use a shave, leave a little around my mouth and on my chin. I put my thumbs through my front belt loops and throw my weight on my back leg.

"They'll stay in there till harvest time if we don't find them," he explains. "Plenty of corn and plenty of water in the wheel tracks. Got no reason to come out."

If he hires Josh and Eric out for an extended period, they'll likely hunt for those cows early morning to dark until the job is done. Spend their days circling all this corn on horseback, switching off walking through the corn-rows, ears and eyes constantly alert, roping any cow they happen to flush out. I can imagine the days starting to look like all this corn, long yellow green days. Pretty soon a day looks like a month and what happened a month ago looks like just the other day.

I watched Eric and Josh rope a bunch of cows just the other day. I found these cowboys on Craigslist in the services section. Their post read COWBOYS FOR HIRE with their names and phone numbers; no emails, no last names. Simple. I could feel myself regressing back to that young Texas boy—*Cow-boys!*—as I waited for Josh to answer the phone, and I began pacing like a kid on a sugar rush. Not two minutes into the phone call and Josh was inviting me out to his place, right then, to watch them in action.

"Get here by six, and you won't miss anything," Josh had said. It was already 5:30, so I dropped everything and drove out to Loveland from Fort Collins. Josh has a practice rodeo arena on his property. By the end of that evening, I was slapping hides and pushing the cows through what's called an approach—an enclosed metal run like a tight hallway that leads to the chute where the cows twist and knock their horns against the gate, waiting for it to open. Once I got a cow into the chute, I waited ready on a nod from Josh, the header, to slam my fist down on a latch that opened the gate and the cow would tear out into the arena. I watched the cowboys rope what's called a flink of cows—an even dozen.

"I *throw* the rope," Josh told me. "The heeler *places* the rope. He needs to get up so close he can do surgery on that cow's behind."

"He ropes around the horns," Eric had said. "I try around the feet. We'll show you this time."

The first three cows were a miss on Eric's part. Heeler's the job of the two that takes more finesse than aggression. But then there was a moment that made me feel like I was in a nineteenth-century oil painting: Josh, on top of his horse Moonshine, yanking the reins hard left, pulling his lasso to tighten the loop and force the cow's head to its shoulder. Eric, leaning forward on Mama—the horse lowering her head to the ground, threads of muscle in her neck and shoulders like lines etched into her black coat. Eric had dropped the lasso for the cow to step into and Mama reared off her front legs. The cow's legs came up off the ground, dust everywhere, and the sun dropped behind the continental divide.

* * *

Now I'm hoping one of Farmer John's cows will come wandering out of the cornrows so I can see Eric and Josh do their thing. I follow him and Josh; me on foot, them on their horses. Josh called about the cow hunt about an hour ago while I was biking home from school. I should have come straight out, but I stopped at Jax Farm & Ranch to buy my new pair of boots, not having boots being the sole reason Josh wouldn't let me ride the other night.

"Get hurt with your tennis shoes slipping through the stirrups," he had said. "It's a rule my dad taught me when I was four. Never ride without boots." So I took an extra thirty minutes and missed the cowboys flushing out and roping and leading two cows to the horse trailer.

"There could be ten cows in the rows," Josh tells me.

"How many cows are there altogether?"

"Twelve. I think it's twelve."

When I was twelve, I dressed a lot like Josh and Eric: cowboy hat, boots and jeans, western shirts, huge belt buckles. This was before I moved to Dallas and enrolled in Apollo Jr. High, where I found out being a roper—would have preferred cowboy, but it was ropers, preppies, freaks, and jocks—wasn't cool. I was the only kid walking those school halls all cowboyed up. My Stetson seemed huge compared to everybody's little heads, and I got looks. I'd like to say I didn't give in, was a nonconformist, but I traded in my look for rock T-shirts and tennis shoes, even changed my Kenny Rogers records out for Def Leppard.

Josh asks if I brought a long-sleeve shirt. "Dammit!" I say. First the boots, now the shirt. He doesn't seem to think it's such a big deal. He loans me his shirt: standard issue cowboy, baby blue cotton collared shirt with pearl snaps, same kind Eric wears. I feel like that kid in the old Coke commercial when he gives Mean Joe Greene a Coke and Mean Joe throws him his sweaty jersey. I put on Josh's shirt and it smells like sweat and too much cologne, there's some horse in there as well. He says to pick a row and walk it and look for cows and push them out on the north side.

"Will I need to slap their asses?"

"No, they'll just move away from you."

Josh shakes his head, sort of smiles, and I feel like maybe I enjoy slapping the cows' asses too much—the quick touch of animal heat on my hand, the dull thud like a baseball hitting a catcher's mitt. A cowboy's job, or so I've always thought, is to drive cattle, brand cows, rope cows, slap their asses, and share a cold beer after a hard day's work. I guess I can say *git* and other cowboy things when I see a cow, but that's not as cowboy as a good hand slap on hide. Maybe I'm not sure what cowboy means.

I head into the corn.

Me and my best friend, Jay, we were cowboys. This was before Apollo, Dallas, the big city, all that. We rode huge wooden reels that were formerly wrapped with big thick wires, cable wires or telephone wires. We found the reels empty of their wires at a construction site in our neighborhood, and we each took one of our own, kept them in our garages. It took some time, but we learned to ride them. We walked the giant reels with ropers, a differ-ent kind of cowboy boot—leather shoes with rubber soles and leather shoe strings; for us, ropers were equal to boots as standard cowboy footwear. When you're up on the round horse, which is what we called them, you walk backward to go forward and forward to go back. We walked our Sachse, Texas, neighborhood up and down and back to front on our round horses because we were cowboys.

I walk miles in the corn. Maybe not miles, but hours. A human, in great shape, can run twenty-six miles in five or less hours. As the crow flies? Who gives a shit? Twenty-six miles is twenty-six miles. If Farmer John enters twelve cows in the Boston Marathon, how many cows are hiding in the cornfield?

"Nine," says Farmer John.

Even though Farmer John's calculations plus the amount roped and trailered equal eleven, when Josh says there are twelve, he does it with this authoritative dead-on-at-you look. His eyes, bright hard blue, tend to fix on a point—that point might be the eyes of the town man he's talking to or the poll between the cow's horns when he's reining back Moonshine with one hand and winding up for the throw. His body seems to lean into that point. I'd almost bet on Josh knowing more about how many cows Farmer John has than Farmer John himself.

Josh is the younger of the two cowboys—twenty-nine to Eric's thirty-two. When he stands, he stands like a wood plank, like what you'd feel okay holding up your barn, say, if you lived in a barn. Josh and Eric can both take a steer by the horns to the ground with their bare hands. I'm talking a thousand-plus-pound beast.

I'd like to say that when I was kid, dressing like a cowboy and listening to cowboy songs, that I was tough like a cowboy, too. I remember standing in front of the mirror and delivering Dirty Harry lines to my reflection. "Feel lucky, punk?" Even had the Eastwood snarl down pat.

One time, I think we were twelve, Jay said something mean to my girlfriend, Tiffany, who lived across the street from me. I don't remember what he said and can't say I was ever sure he'd said anything. What I do remember is calling him up, Jay, who was tall and lanky and had a long reach—something like what I imagine Josh to have looked like as a kid—and asking him to meet me in the street halfway between my house and his. I didn't tell him what it was about. He rode up on his bike, and I walked up, and he said *what?* I punched him, catching him on the chin, then I turned and ran home. I hadn't handled the situation like a cowboy. Jay did, though. He took that punch and never said anything about it, never tried to get me back, though I don't remember us walking round horses together after that. I had cried, wished I hadn't run back to the safety of the house where there was a brick wall separating me from the only other cowboy I knew at the time.

My new boots get covered in mud as I walk the wheel tracks and search for cows. I see cow tracks all over—twin sets of ovals in the mud—but no cows. The leaves of the cornstalks sometimes rattle behind me, where I just nudged them, and it's startling. I look back with a jerk, worried it might be an angry cow. My hands dry up and have tiny red lines of scratches from parting stalks. The corn looks good though, gives off a smell not unlike sweet grass. I walk around the wheel tracks and cross through rows when it gets too muddy. I have no idea where I am. I walk for a good hour down one track, bending over at each row and looking left and right, putting a lot of strain on my lower back. I can't imagine doing this all day long.

I've learned from Farmer John that the wheel tracks are made by sprinkler towers fed by the pivot pond. (Pivot pond: just a plain ole pond used as a water supply for the irrigation system.) The towers run circles through the cornfield, so this wheel track could just be winding me deeper into the corn, and it's nearing sundown, and if I don't get out soon, then what? I hear a cow lowing somewhere to my right. It sounds more like a drawn-out groan than a moo. I leave the track and head down a row in that direction. The closer I get, the more the sound seems to be coming from my left, so I cross rows in that direction and then the mooing sounds like it's somewhere to my right. I bend down and look to my right, to my left. I don't see the cow anywhere. The lowing stops. I head to the wheel track and follow it back the way I came.

Josh calls me on my cell. "Pick a row and head west," he says. "Come out on the west side. That's where we are." I look up, around; it's nothing but sky and corn. How the hell am I supposed to know west from anything else? The sun is setting but it's difficult to tell where the light is exactly; it covers too much area. I pick a row and head to where the light seems to be strongest. I've given up on looking for cows; no more bending over, my back aches, so I cross my arms at the wrists and hold them up high in front of me to keep the tassels from slapping and itching my face.

The other day, I got to see the cowboys rope some steers, too. It was more like what they'd be doing out here. They had let two steers out into the open of the arena—no approach, no chute. It was dusk, around the same time it is now, when they brought out the steers.

"We'll pretend they haven't seen people for a while," Eric had said. "They're kind of spunky."

The steers were much larger than the cows, one white and one red. Unlike bulls, steers have been castrated, but that lower level of testosterone doesn't seem to calm them down much. As soon as they were let into the arena, they went head to head, whacking horns and it sounded like a baseball bat striking a ball.

Me and Jay played baseball every summer that I lived in Sachse. One summer, Jay constantly chewed toothpicks when he was playing, and so did I. I thought it looked pretty cool and maybe kind of cowboy, like you might think of a man out in a pasture with a peduncle wheat stem between his teeth. Maybe that's more a farmer thing. The toothpicks were hot fire cinnamon that stayed with you after you spit one out, and we kept chewing them when we went back to school that fall.

Other kids thought it was cool and started chewing flavored toothpicks at school, too. Pretty soon kids were soaking regular toothpicks in various kinds of extract—pecan, root beer, pumpkin spice, vanilla. One kid even started soaking them in whiskey and sold them for a quarter apiece. Toothpicks became outlawed at school. This was Webb Middle School, before Apollo, before I sucker-punched Jay and we stopped riding round horses. I quit chewing cinnamon toothpicks to stay out of trouble. Jay didn't. He wasn't about to bow down to authority—he was a cowboy. When I moved to Dallas and turned in my cowboy clothes, changed from roper to freak, I wondered if Jay still wore big belt buckles and chewed cinnamon toothpicks. I thought about him up at bat chewing one of those toothpicks while I watched the steers and listened to the cracks of their horns.

"Are they playing?" I asked Eric.

"Right now," he said. "But that could change."

That's what the cowboys were doing that night—playing. But that could change, too. The reason they had brought out the steers was to give me a better idea of what it's like when they get called out on a job.

"A rancher might call us up to come out and rope some wild cows," Eric said. "It could be on hundreds or thousands of acres, and that's a lot of room to move."

I watched as Eric and Josh rode after the large red steer. There was maybe a tenth of sun cresting over the top of Longs Peak, and it was getting difficult to see. Josh finally got close enough and threw the noose over the steer's horns, turning the steer hard left and slowing it down. Eric came up behind, placed the rope on the ground at the steer's hind legs, but only got one leg. Mama reared back. Eric jumped off, ran to the steer, grabbed it by the horns, and forced it down with all his weight. I ran over, and Eric was breathing hard, his shirt soaked in sweat and a darker shade of blue in the dim light.

Josh dismounted and walked over to the steer and showed me how the animal's two back legs and one front leg, closest to the ground, were hogtied with piggin' string. "They can stay like this for maybe three hours before they die. You want to make sure the horse trailer isn't too far away so they're still alive by the time you get back." Cows and steers can't breathe well when tied up like this and they'll eventually suffocate.

Josh untied the steer and then showed me this neat trick. "When on the job, you can't know every cow's or steer's temperament. I don't want him jumping up and charging me while I'm still on foot." He grabbed the lip of skin at the top of the steer's hind leg. "What you do is you grab it here by the flank." With all his strength, he rocked the steer back and forth maybe half-a-dozen times, appearing to massage its underside and lower back. Then he stood up and the steer lay there, very calm. "You see that?" he said. "He'll lay there for a while and give me time to saddle." Josh mounted up and then whistled at the steer. The steer hopped up and walked away.

As I head out of the corn, I wonder if Farmer John knows as much about cows as these cowboys do. I come out of the cornfield on the northwest side and hear Josh yell that west is this way, where he is. I follow Josh north and then east around the corn.

"Farmers have no business owning cows," Josh says.

"'Cause they can hide in the corn?" I ask.

"Good a reason as any."

He tells me they got three cows altogether and there are still nine missing. That makes a flink. I look at his boots and they're so covered in mud you can't see one speck of leather. Mine look pretty clean in comparison.

"Seems like it'll be hard to find them in all that corn," I say.

"I don't think there's any more cows in the corn," Josh tells me. "Most likely they crossed the fence line and are on somebody else's property. Problem is, they're not branded, and if they mix in with the neighbor's cows, that's it."

The day's cow hunt is over. We stand outside the horse trailer in the head-lights of Eric's truck.

Josh deals out bottles of Bud Light. Farmer John puts his hand up and shakes his head. I gladly accept and Josh smiles. "Good man," he says.

ECHO KLAPROTH

Calving Time

As the oldest of four siblings and the only girl, I grew up under unusual circumstances. The ranch was seventy-five miles from the nearest town, and it was nine miles to the closest neighbor's. I went to school with my three brothers in our "backyard," and because I preferred being outdoors, spent any spare time with Dad and a bevy of hired men; I was rarely indoors with Mom. I'm not sure when Dad and I became fully cognizant of the fact that I wasn't one of the "boys." I'm now speculating it happened in the spring of my twelfth year, during calving time.

* * *

We found her on our four o'clock ride through the herd. Dad noticed her first: acting nervous, circling, with blood and slime dripping from her behind—all the signs of imminent birth. We decided to take her in, but confirming the impetuousness of youth and inexperience, she ran every direction but toward the barn which offered a comfortable straw bed, four walls, and a roof overhead—protection from the cold and elements peculiar to a Wyoming April. Frustrated with her defiance, Dad finally roped her around the neck, and with that and my rope tugging on her tender rump, we coerced her progress in the direction she needed to go. She strained against the ropes all the way, only and finally falling in defeat after we dragged her into the sanctity of the barn.

"She's damned young to be so stubborn," Dad grumbled.

As she lay on the ground, her sides heaved with calf and struggle. Fear formed white sweat foam that coated her entire bulk, and her tail whipped like a flag in a frequently changing head wind. She reeked of urine, manure, birth, and terror. Dad went to work, because as he'd often explained, "Time is of the essence during a birthing." Impatiently he told me to "get out of the way" as he tied her hind feet to one end of the stall and front ones to the opposite wall. I watched her eyes alter from black and white to bloody pink as they rolled; she was bound securely to a uterus that was attempting to rupture every few minutes.

"She's scared, huh, Dad?"

"Yeah," he muttered while throwing off his coat and rolling up his right sleeve. Dad knelt and pushed his arm hard into the heifer's cervix. Anticipating what was to happen next, I ran to get the calf pullers. On my return to the stall, I found Dad swearing out loud at the young cow. "Dammit to hell, you're too young to be in this kind of a jam. I'll be lucky to save you or your baby."

He grabbed the steel calving tool from me and with one motion latched the chain around the one protruding foot he could reach outside the cow's vulva and began working the pulley lever.

"This is my fault. I should'a been watchin' closer," he told her. Over his shoulder he spoke to me. "Remember when Turner's bull got in the yearlin's early? I didn't think he'd done any damage. This is what I get for not payin' attention."

Both his hands and words flew fast and furious. I backed against the wall, feeling a sudden and unexplainable knot tighten in my stomach. "Is this what Mom was talkin' about when she told me about havin' babies too young?" I asked.

The Hereford bellowed in agonizing response with each crank of the pulley. Suddenly, Dad burst out, "This isn't doing any good; that other leg must be turned back." He yanked the chain from the calf's foot and kicked the birthing device across the floor.

I ventured, "What do we do now, Dad?"

He whirled around looking me square in the face as if seeing me for the first time that day. His wild eyes and furrowed brow said, *I don't know.* His mouth spit out, "We gotta let 'er up and see if she can do it on her own." And while we untied first her front legs and then her hind, he stammered, "We gotta see if she can do it on her own."

A rancher his whole life, Dad always managed with confidence built on a lifetime of experience. Now he seemed in a daze. This was the first time I'd seen him confused. I felt uncomfortable. When he finally spoke, it was in a stern tone, and I remember thinking he was looking right through me. "Yes! To answer your question." And then more gently, "Yes. This is exactly what your mother was talkin' about."

I wished I could go to the house and be with her.

He lit a cigarette and drew deeply on it, motioning for me to step away. "Let's give 'er some room." I watched smoke curl toward the hayloft as we moved over to a dark corner of the barn, watching while the heifer tried to get up.

Her plaintive groan with each effort confirmed Dad's spoken fear. "She's too weak." Throwing down the cigarette, he ran to her hind end and once again dropped to his knees. "Help me," he said, and I thought he sounded scared. I moved to his side, wanting to make things all right.

For what seemed an eternity, we wrestled—the cow, Dad, and me—together and alone. Dad was trying to turn the calf, and he had me massaging the outside of the heifer's belly. The young Hereford seemed to sense we were trying to help her and had quit struggling against us. Our every action was tied to the heaving inside her.

And then everything stopped. With one long, anguished moan the heavy breathing stopped; all contortions stopped; the full, round belly collapsed. I knew she was dead and was surprised that Dad didn't yet seem to realize it. He was still pulling on the calf.

"Dad? Dad, I think she's dead."

He looked up and slowly pulled his arms away from her. They fell limp to his lap. His head dropped. He pushed his hat back and rubbed the back of his wrist across his sweaty forehead. I found myself wanting to go and hug him but wondered why; we'd lost cows before.

And then our eyes met. "She was too young to have to go through this. She shouldn't have had to go through this. People make choices. She was just a dumb animal. She didn't have a choice." He looked small and helpless, sad, and very tired. At that moment I silently vowed I would never get pregnant. And I knew it as sure as I knew anything. I never wanted to see my dad like this again. I could hardly wait to talk to Mom.

CONTRIBUTORS

Contributor Notes

Gina Marie Bernard lives in Bemidji, Minnesota, where she teaches high school English. When not writing, she slips into her alter ego, wicked vixen, a blocker for the Babe City Rollers roller derby team. She is the crazy-proud parent of two beautiful daughters, Maddie and Parker. Her work appears or is forthcoming in several journals, including *Glitterwolf, Aperion Review, Milk Sugar, Sinister Wisdom*, and *Collective Fallout*. Her young adult novel, *Alpha Summer*, is available at LOONFEATHERPRESS.COM.

Michelle Bonczek is the author of *The Art of the Nipple* (Orange Monkey Publishing, 2013). Her poems have appeared widely in journals, including *Crazyhorse, cream city review, Green Mountains Review, Orion, & Water~Stone Review*. She holds a Ph.D. from Western Michigan University and an MFA from Eastern Washington University. She is an avid gardener and photographer, and teaches writing in Syracuse, New York.

Allen Braden is the author of *A Wreath of Down and Drops of Blood* (University of Georgia) and *Elegy in the Passive Voice* (University of Alaska/Fairbanks). His poems have been anthologized by Bedford/St. Martins Press, Harvard Common Press, Texas Review Press and University of Iowa Press. He grew up on a cattle ranch outside White Swan, Washington.

Sally Clark's poetry has been published in *Relief, Weavings, Chrysalis Reader, The Binnacle*, and three years of the *Texas Poetry Calendar*. Her poems have won first place awards from Willamette Writers Kay Snow Poetry Award, Northern Colorado Writers Association, San Antonio Writers Guild, Abilene Writers Guild, and many others. Sally lives in Fredericksburg, Texas. You can find her online at SALLYCLARK.INFO.

Peter Clarke holds a BA in Psychology from Western Washington University and recently completed his JD at the University of the Pacific, McGeorge School of Law. His short fiction has appeared in *Hobart, Elimae, Pif Magazine, Curbside Splendor, Denver Syntax, Pure Francis, Zygote in my Coffee*, and elsewhere. Native to Port Angeles, Washington, he currently lives in Sacramento, California.

F. Brett Cox's fiction, poetry, essays, and reviews have appeared in numerous publications. With Andy Duncan, he co-edited the anthology *Crossroads:*

Tales of the Southern Literary Fantastic (Tor, 2004). A native of North Carolina, Brett is Associate Professor of English at Norwich University and lives in Vermont with his wife, playwright Jeanne Beckwith.

David Lavar Coy lived and worked on a farm in Wyoming when young, earned an MFA in Creative Writing from the University of Arkansas in Fayetteville, and directed the creative writing program at Arizona Western College in Yuma for nineteen years. His poetry books are *Rural News*, *Lean Creatures*, and *Down Time to Tombstone* (with poems also by David Tammer).

Carolyn Dahl's writing has appeared in *Women and Poetry: Tips on Writing, Teaching and Publishing* (McFarland), *Copper Nickel*, *Hawai'i Review*, *Camas*, *Colere*, and twenty-four anthologies. She was a finalist award winner in nonfiction in PEN Texas Literary Competition, serves on the board of Mutabilis Poetry Press, is the author of *Natural Impressions* (Watson-Guptill) and *Transforming Fabric* (Krause/F&W Books). She has raised monarch butterflies in her Houston kitchen for about ten years.

Heather Fowler is the author of the story collections *Suspended Heart* (Aqueous Books, 2010), *People With Holes* (Pink Narcissus Press, 2012) and *This Time, While We're Awake* (Aqueous Books, forthcoming Spring 2013). Her work has been published online and in print in the U.S., England, Australia, and India. Visit her website: HEATHERFOWLERWRITES.COM

Carol Guerrero-Murphy is a professor at Adams State University in Alamosa, Colorado. She continues to play cowboy with her old sweet mustang Lucky and the herd of several other rowdy horses he lives with. Her first collection of poetry, *Table Walking at Nighthawk* (Ghost Road Press, 2007) was awarded a WILLA (Women Writing the West) Award.

Lyla D. Hamilton's writing often reflects her Western roots and her interest in the human-animal bond. She has published prose and poetry, and has earned awards from the Professional Writers of Prescott (Arizona) and the Carnegie Center, Lexington, Kentucky. Lyla holds a Ph.D. in philosophy from UCLA and lives near Boulder, Colorado, with canines Wookie and Luke Skywalker.

Merrill Shane Jones lives in Denver with his wife, Michele, and dog, Maxine—two cowgirls from Texas. He is a graduate of the Colorado State University Creative Writing MFA program and is working on two novels about cowpunchers, outlaws, and U.S. Marshals. His stories appear or are forthcoming in *Gulf Stream, Main Street Rag,* and elsewhere.

Donna Kaz is a poet and lyricist whose poems have been published in *Lilith, Trivia,* and *Step Away Magazine* (Pushcart Prize Nomination.) She is the recipient of residency fellowships from Yaddo, Djerassi, Blue Mountain, Ucross and the New Lyric Institute for New Musicals. She resides in New York City. Her Twitter handle is @DONNAKAZ.

Poet and essayist **Rick Kempa** teaches writing and directs the Honors Program at Western Wyoming College in Rock Springs, Wyoming. *Ten Thousand Voices,* his second book of poems, was published in 2013 by Littoral Press.

Echo Klaproth is a fourth generation Wyoming rancher, writer, retired teacher and ordained minister. Her writing reflects the stories of her family's heritage; the struggles, gains, and growth as a woman, wife, mother, friend, and Christian, as well as the blessings she celebrates because she was born and raised in Wyoming, among good and honest folks.

Klipschutz (pen name of Kurt Lipschutz) is a poet, songwriter and journalist. His most recent book of poems is *This Drawn & Quartered Moon* (Anvil Press, 2013). Previous books include *Twilight of the Male Ego* and *The Erection of Scaffolding for the Re-Painting of Heaven by the Lowest Bidder.* He lives in San Francisco, California.

Tricia Knoll is a Portland, Oregon, poet who spent many summers riding in Colorado's mountains, wanting to be a cowgirl. She maintains friendships with horses . . . and a dog. Her poetry, appearing in national and regional journals, often focuses on human interactions with urban wildlife.

Ellaraine Lockie is a widely published and awarded poet, nonfiction book author, and essayist. Her recent work has been awarded the 2013 Women's National Book Association's Poetry Prize, Best Individual Collection from *Purple Patch Magazine* in England, winner of the San Gabriel Poetry Festival Chapbook Contest, and The Aurorean's 2012 Chapbook Spring Pick.

Coffee House Confessions was recently released from Silver Birch Press. She also teaches poetry workshops and serves as Poetry Editor for the lifestyles magazine *Lilipoh*.

John McCarthy is the Assistant Editor of *Quiddity International Literary Journal* and Public Radio Program. His work has appeared in the *Conium Review*, *Popshot Magazine* (UK), *Buddhist Poetry Review*, and *Ghost Ocean Magazine's* Wave Series, among other journals and anthologies. When not writing, he coaches cross country and distance track at Benedictine University in Springfield. He can be contacted at JJMCCARTHY90@GMAIL.COM.

Anna Moore is a poet, a creator of small fictions, an editor at *Routledge*, and an inarticulate pursuer of the ineffable. Major interests include books and their futures, literacy and psychology, the collection and dissemination of information, and the construction and structure of meaning. Anna is from Denver, Colorado, and resides in both Providence, Rhode Island, and Brooklyn, New York.

William Notter is the author of *Holding Everything Down* (Southern Illinois University Press, 2009), winner of the 2010 High Plains Book Award for Poetry, and finalist for the Colorado Book Award. He holds an MFA from the University of Arkansas. His poems have appeared on NPR's *The Writer's Almanac* and in journals, including *Alaska Quarterly*, *AGNI*, *Crab Orchard Review* and *High Desert Journal*.

Stephen Page is the author of *The Timbre of Sand* and *Still Dandelions*. He holds a BA from Columbia University and an MFA from Bennington College. He is the recipient of The Jess Cloud Memorial Prize for Poetry. He loves to travel, teach, ranch, and spend time with his family. All characters, places, and events in this poem are fictitious.

Robert Rebein is the author of *Dragging Wyatt Earp: A Personal History of Dodge City* (Athens: Swallow/Ohio U Press, 2013) and *Hicks, Tribes, & Dirty Realists: American Fiction After Postmodernism* (Lexington: U Kentucky Press, 2001). He teaches creative writing and directs the graduate English program at Indiana University Purdue University in Indianapolis. Reach him at ROBERTREBEIN.COM.

Heather Sappenfield's stories have won the Danahy Fiction Prize, the Arthur Edelstein Prize for Short Fiction, and a Pushcart nomination. They have appeared in *Meridian, So To Speak, Tampa Review, Joyland*, and *Shenandoah*. Her story collection, which includes "Real Cowboy," was a finalist for the Flannery O'Connor Award. Learn more about her writing at HEATHERSAPPENFIELD.COM.

Michael Shay is a Colorado native who lives and works in Cheyenne, Wyoming. His short story collection, *The Weight of a Body*, was published by Ghost Road Press. His work has been published in *Northern Lights, High Plains Literary Review, Colorado Review, Owen Wister Review, Visions, Relief* and *Working Words: Punching the Clock and Kicking out the Jams*.

Tom Sheehan has 330 western stories published in several publications, and one collection, *The Westering*, that was nominated for a National Book Award. His early-day comfort zone in writing is western stories and poems. He has sixteen books to his credit, including an NHL mystery, *Murder at the Forum*, an eBook at AMAZON.COM, and two in the queue at the publisher. Nigh onto his 85th birthday, he keeps his shoulder to the wheel.

Red Shuttleworth is the author of three poetry books (*Western Settings, Johnny Ringo*, and *Ghosts and Birthdays*) and a couple dozen chapbooks. Shuttleworth, a three-time Spur Award for Poetry recipient, was named "Best Living Western Poet" by *True West* magazine in 2007. His poems have appeared in hundreds of journals, including *Concho River Review* and *Los Angeles Review*.

M.R. Smith is a poet and essayist writing in Boise, Idaho. His work has appeared in publications such as *Cascadia Review, Camas, Literary Bohemian, Punchnel's, Red River Review*, and the FutureCycle Press anthology *What Poets See*, among others. He is currently finishing his first poetry collection.

Adam Tavel received the 2010 Robert Frost Award, and his forthcoming collections are *The Fawn Abyss* (Salmon, 2014) and *Red Flag Up* (Kattywompus, 2013), a chapbook of letter-poems. His work has appeared in *West Branch, Indiana Review, Zone 3, South Dakota Review, Minnesota Review*, and *Cincinnati Review*, among others.

Don Thackrey lives in Dexter, Michigan, where he is retired from the University of Michigan. His early years were spent on farms and ranches in the Sandhills of Nebraska. Much of his verse draws upon memories of rural life before modern conveniences. A book of such verse is forthcoming from the Dakota Institute Press.

Sarah Brown-Weitzman, a recipient of National Endowment for the Arts award, has had work in numerous journals and anthologies, including *North American Review, American Writing, Potomac Review, Art Time, Bellingham Review, M.I.T.Rune, Rattle,* and *America.* Her second chapbook was *The Forbidden* (Pudding House, 2004), followed by *Never Far From Flesh,* a full-length volume of poetry (Pure Heart/Main Street Rag, 2005). Her latest book is *Herman and the Ice Witch,* a children's novel (Main Street Rag, 2011). A former New York academic, Weitzman is retired and lives in Florida.

Joe Wilkins is the author of a memoir, *The Mountain and the Fathers: Growing up on the Big Dry,* a 2012 Montana Book Award Honor Book, and two collections of poems, *Notes from the Journey Westward* and *Killing the Murnion Dogs.* He lives with his family in the Yamhill Valley of Western Oregon.

Leonore Wilson lives a rather hermetic life in the wilds of Northern California. Her most fulfilling conversation this week was a nearly ten-minute hi/grr-r chat with a native gray fox (an exceptionally beautiful vixen with a lot on her mind). Leonore taught eighteen years at Napa Valley College and recently had a guest lecturer/professor stint at a private university in San Francisco. Her work has been in *TRIVIA, Quarterly West, MAGMA, Third Coast,* and *Madison Review,* among other literary magazines. She has been awarded fellowships and grants for her writing. Right now, her main priority is to save her fourth generation female-owned ranch from encroaching land grabbers who don't realize water is gold.

Kathleen Winter's first poetry collection, *Nostalgia for the Criminal Past,* won the Antivenom Prize and was published by Elixir Press in 2012. Her poems were published by *Tin House, New Republic, AGNI, Cincinnati Review,* and *FIELD.* Winter was granted fellowships by Vermont Studio Center, Prague Summer Program and Virginia G. Piper Center. She teaches literature and writing at the University of San Francisco.

Brenda Yates is a Pushcart Prize nominee, winner of the Beyond Baroque Poetry Contest, and the Patricia Bibby Memorial Prize. Her work appears in numerous journals including *Mississippi Review, Cider Press Review, Eclipse, Spillway, StepAway* and in *City of the Big Shoulders: An Anthology of Chicago Poetry* (University of Iowa Press) and *The Southern Poetry Anthology, Volume VI: Tennessee* (Texas Review Press).

About the Editors and Designer

Teresa Milbrodt received her MFA in Creative Writing and her MA in American Culture Studies from Bowling Green State University. She is the author of the short story collection *Bearded Women: Stories* (Chizine Publications), the upcoming novel *The Patron Saint of Unattractive People* (Boxfire Press), and the upcoming flash fiction collection *Larissa's Guide to Trying to Be a Good Person in the World*. Milbrodt's stories have appeared in numerous literary journals, and several have been nominated for the Pushcart Prize. She lives in Gunnison, Colorado, with her husband, Tristan, and cat, Aspen.

Michaela Roessner has published four novels, and shorter works in venues including *Asimov's Magazine*, *F&SF*, *OMNI*, *Room* and assorted anthologies. Her novel *Walkabout Woman* won the Crawford and John W. Campbell awards. She's had pieces short-listed for the Calvino Prize, the Tiptree Award, the Mythopoeic Award, and the Millennium Publishing contest. Recent short fiction publications include "The Klepsydra," published in *F&SF* in late 2011, and "The Fishes Speak," in P.S. Publishing's anthology *The Company He Keeps*. She is working on the third novel in a set about Catherine de Medici for Tachyon Publications. She teaches creative writing at Western State Colorado University's low-residency MFA program and online classes for Gotham Writers' Workshop.

With a doctorate in English from Texas Tech University, **Mark Todd** has served on the faculty at Western for twenty-five years, where he serves as program director for Western State Colorado University's MFA in Creative Writing and also teaches undergraduate creative writing. His own works include two collections of poetry (*Wire Song*, 2001; *Tamped, But Loose Enough to Breathe*, 2008), and three novels—two paranormal adventure-comedies co-written with wife Kym O'Connell-Todd (*Little Greed Men*, 2006, 2013; *All Plucked Up*, 2012) and one science fiction novel (*Strange Attractors*, 2012). He and his wife are currently at work on book three of the Silverville Saga, *The Magicke Outhouse*, forthcoming in early 2014. He also has a narrative nonfiction book forthcoming.

David Yezzi's books of poems include *Azores* (2008) and *Birds of the Air* (2013). He is editor of *The Swallow Anthology of New American Poets* and executive editor of *The New Criterion*. He lives in New York City.

Sonya Unrein is the editorial director for Conundrum Press, which is the literary imprint of Samizdat Publishing Group. She was a founding owner of Denver's Ghost Road Press, where she won the Colorado Book Award for best anthology in 2006. She is also a freelance editor, book designer, and publishing consultant for authors and small presses. She has an M.A. from the University of Denver in Digital Media Studies and lives in a Denver suburb.